Linda Aronson was born and brought up in London and decided to write after a brief career as the worst tea lady ever. She now lives in Sydney with her husband and has two children. She works full-time as an author, playwright and screenwriter, as well as lecturing on the business.

Naturally Rude is the third hilarious book about Ian Rude and his outrageous escapades. The previous two, *Rude Health* and *Plain Rude*, were published to rave reviews, some of which are listed below:

'Hilarious . . . constant entertainment' *Guardian*

'A truly funny book' *The Times*

'Linda Aronson is one of the best comic writers . . . another first-rate tale' *Daily Telegraph*

'To laugh yourself stupid, pick up *Rude Health*' *Girlfriend*

'Aronson uses humour to explore without ever belittling the concerns of young adults' *Daily Telegraph* (Australia)

Also by Linda Aronson

The first two Ian Rude books:
Rude Health
Plain Rude

Kelp

'I'm a huge fan . . . one of the funniest books ever.
Aronson is the mistress of spiralling frenetic climax'
Mary Hoffman, *Armadillo*

'quite hilarious' *Mail on Sunday*

'The pace, wit and bizarreness are delightful'
Guardian

LINDA ARONSON

Naturally RUDE

OR HOW TO HAVE A MEANINGFUL
RELATIONSHIP WHEN SOMEONE'S
STICKING A SCREWDRIVER
UP YOUR NOSE

MACMILLAN CHILDREN'S BOOKS

First published 2007 by Macmillan Children's Books
a division of Macmillan Publishers Limited
20 New Wharf Road, London N1 9RR
Basingstoke and Oxford
www.panmacmillan.com

Associated companies throughout the world

ISBN: 978-0-330-48255-4

1 3 5 7 9 8 6 4 2

A CIP catalogue record for this book is available from
the British Library.

Typeset by Intype Libra Limited
Printed and bound in Great Britain by Mackays of Chatham plc, Kent

Grateful thanks to Ruth Alltimes at
Macmillan's Children Books, UK,
Dmetri Kakmi and Laura Harris at Penguin Australia,
and Geoffrey Radford of Anthony Williams Agency.
Very special thanks, as ever, to my family

1

I'm in serious trouble.

It's the start of the holidays, I'm starving and I'm stuck in an up-market boutique in our shopping mall. Any moment now my girlfriend, Tash, is going to come out of the changing cubicle wearing an evening dress. I've got to give her my opinion on whether this dress is right for her to wear when she plays the piano at a big youth orchestra concert at the Town Hall in two weeks' time.

The problem is, this dress is about the sixteenth one she's tried on and they all look exactly the same.

To make things worse, anything I say is likely to be taken as a criticism of Tash's figure. Even breathing in a certain way is a criticism of Tash's figure. And not saying *anything* is the worst criticism of all.

Honestly, Tash normally is this happy, good-looking, super-smart Year 9 who, as it happens, is also a musical genius. What I've just discovered is that once she goes shopping for dresses, she turns into a mad-eyed, tight-lipped psycho who keeps giving little shrieks of rage and crashing in and out of changing rooms.

It turns out that in moods like this she thinks she's a hot-air balloon with bad hair, and nothing I can say will persuade her otherwise. In fact, everything I say will be taken down and used in evidence against me. Even if I specifically tell her she isn't fat, she thinks I'm just saying that to cover up that I think she is. In fact, the F word is a total disaster area. That other F word is nothing in comparison. The real F word can mean your life is a misery for days.

And don't think you're off the hook by never actually saying it either. No way. You've got to keep your entire conversation away from the business of weight altogether.

Don't ask me why someone as super-intelligent as Tash can obsess over something as stupid as this. It's a mystery. But she does.

To be honest, I find girls difficult, and it's not only the F thing. I'm not sexist. It's just that sometimes I have real trouble understanding them, and I keep putting my foot in it. OK, Tash is my first girlfriend, but we've been going out for three months, so you'd think I'd be up to speed on what makes her tick.

No way.

As fast as I get myself out of one tricky situation I get myself into another. It's not that I don't try to get it right. I do. I really want to make her happy. I think she's gorgeous. She's smart, she's funny, she's hot. If she ever broke up with me I'd be beyond gutted and, I have to say, I don't really know what she sees in me.

But, seriously, sometimes it's like she comes from a different planet.

For example, last week. We're sitting on the wharf overlooking some fishing boats and the sun's setting. The sky's all red and gold.

And she says, 'What are you thinking?'

So I say, truthfully, 'I was just thinking that if the Panthers beat the Crows they're into the semis.'

She looks at me like I'd blown my nose on the tablecloth at my granny's birthday party.

What I've now realized is that at any time of the day or night, girls are always thinking something deep. But (and I don't think girls actually get this) boys, unless there's something serious or funny happening, aren't really thinking about much at all. They're kind of just ticking over. If they're happy, they're just happily ticking over.

So, if you ask a girl, 'What are you thinking?' you'll get five minutes' precise description of how she's feeling today, how she was feeling yesterday and how she's likely to feel tomorrow. Also, she'll be really pleased you asked. But if you ask a boy what he's thinking, he's likely to look at you suspiciously and say, 'Nothing.' Alternatively he might say, 'Whadda *you* thinking about, dog breath?' and bop you one.

But I'm learning. Basically, if a girl asks her boyfriend what he's thinking it's because she wants him to be romantic and meaningful. So, even if all you're thinking is something sort of happily aimless

3

like, 'If I had a pine cone I could peg that bird right off that branch' (not that you'd do it, you're just kind of vaguely thinking it), you don't say that. And whatever you do, you don't say, 'Nothing,' because then she'll assume you're doing what a girl would, which is having deep, dark thoughts about your life that you're dying to talk about but are nobly keeping to yourself. What happens then is that she'll pester you for half an hour to tell her these thoughts, and when it turns out all you were really thinking about was causing grievous bodily harm to a dumb animal, she looks at you like you're some kind of Neanderthal.

The trick is, give half the truth. So you say, 'I was thinking about the bird sitting on that fence.' This way, she thinks you're really poetic and thoughtful. And you're safe.

Another good one is, 'I was just thinking how cool it is to be with you.' Which would be true if you were actually thinking about anything, instead of just staring blankly into space.

If you think I'm a male chauvinist because I'm saying all this, honestly I'm not. I'm crazy about Tash. I just want to make her happy. All I wish is that it was a bit easier to work her out. And I really wish there wasn't an issue about the F word. She's perfect. The whole obsession about her weight is completely ridiculous. Not to mention exhausting, because I never know when I'm going to say the wrong thing.

I shift uneasily on the yellow silk couch. I stare

down at my battered Nikes, then up at the racks of beaded, shiny dresses. Every dress in this shop is covered in plastic. The shop assistant is looking at me like she's wishing she could wrap me in plastic. Like some sort of antibacterial garbage bag. On top of everything else, I'm starving. I didn't have time for breakfast and we started out at eight thirty. I've lost count of the number of dress shops we've been in since then. Even worse, I've got a big juicy half-eaten kebab rolled in pitta bread in the inside pocket of my jacket – I bought it between shops – but I don't dare get it out because there's a big sign next to me saying: 'No food to be eaten on the premises', and the way that shop assistant's looking at me, one glimpse of a kebab and she'll call the military.

My stomach makes a loud whirring sound. The shop assistant raises an eyebrow, then heads off up the shop and ducks down to sort boxes under the counter.

I think longingly of the kebab. It's a double size, with lettuce, tomatoes, barbecued meat, fried onions and, the final touch, a big dollop of sauce. My mouth actually waters. If the shop assistant would only go out the back, I could sneak a bite. Mind you, she's taking a very long time with those boxes under the counter.

I could have a quick mouthful now . . .

Super-casually, I slither my hand inside my jacket, whip out the kebab, take a big bite and hastily stuff it back in my pocket again.

Ah . . . Even the smell's lovely.

I'm munching happily when the shop assistant suddenly pops up, sniffs the air and glares at me. I'm frozen mid-chew, my mouth stuffed. I give her a wide, closed-lipped smile.

She frowns and snaps, 'You'd better not be eating in here. I don't want stains on my new couch.'

I grin brightly with my mouth clamped shut, bobbing my head about, as if eating is so far from my mind I find it funny. She gives me another suspicious look and ducks down behind the counter again.

Old bag.

I swallow luxuriously, sneak the kebab out again, take another enormous bite – and a big jet of sauce and two bits of fried onion shoot out of the bottom and land on the couch.

Oh no!

I stick the kebab back in my pocket, flick the onion on to the carpet and brush the stain with my hand. It spreads into a big teardrop shape. Why did I do that? I start rubbing it frantically. It looks even worse. Now it's the size of a CD. This is terrible.

Right at that moment the shop assistant bobs up with a shoe box. I freeze, my mouth still stuffed. What am I going to do? I've just wrecked her couch. She's coming over. She's going to see it.

I quickly shift sideways to sit on the stain and clamp my shoe over the onion. The problem is, the onion's a metre away from the couch, so I have to stick my leg out with a pointed toe, like I'm about to launch off into some kind of ballet dance.

At exactly that moment Tash teeters out of the cubicle in a black dress. And there's a problem.

It's not that I can't tell this dress from all the others. I wish.

The problem is, the dress is way too small for her and it's got a rigid strapless top that she's bursting out of. Put it this way, one bout of hiccups and she'd be arrested. But I can't say that or she'll think I'm saying she's (don't say it) f-a-t.

'What do you think?' She turns round and adjusts her hair.

I gasp. As she holds her arms up, the top part of the dress is so stiff the front of it juts right out. You can see straight down inside it. People could start chucking peanuts in there.

'I said, what do you think?'

I shift the kebab into my cheek and mumble brightly, 'It's black!'

'Is that a problem?'

'No. You look . . .' I struggle, '. . . really hot.'

She bristles. 'Hot? It's a classical concert.'

'I mean . . . elegant.'

Luckily, she turns to the mirror – even better, the shop assistant goes over to her, so I can dip down and snatch up the onion.

'You don't think it's too long?'

I shift the kebab into my other cheek.

'What do *you* think?'

Here's another tip. You can usually avoid trouble just by asking the same question back. But this time I can't wriggle out of the problem. This is serious. I've got to stop her buying this dress.

She spins in front of the mirror.

'I like it. And you know, it's a size smaller than I usually wear – what d'you think of these buttons?'

They're buttons. What can you say about buttons? The question is whether you'll hit a chord and your boobs'll pop out.

I'm playing for time. 'What do *you* think of the buttons?'

'I'm not sure. Which d'you like the best, this dress or the blue one?'

I think quickly. 'The blue one. I liked the buttons.'

'The blue one didn't have any buttons. The blue one had a bow. *This* one's got the buttons.'

But she's stopped. She's staring over her shoulder at her reflection, frowning. Her eyes are narrowing. One eyebrow's lifting . . .

'You don't think it makes me look . . . *fat*?'

Oh no.

I beam. 'Nah!'

'But my bum *does* look big.'

What am I supposed to say? Her bum *does* look big. But it always looks big. It *is* big. It's magnificent. It's one of the best things about her figure.

My grin's fixed. 'No way.'

She's glaring. 'Don't tell me what you think I want to hear. My bum looks big in this, right?'

'I liked the neckline on that green one.'

'I didn't ask you that.' Her eyes are burning. 'I asked you, *does my bum look big in this?*'

She's glaring at me. The shop assistant's glaring at me. Any minute they're going to discover I've wrecked the couch – and on top of that, we're now speeding towards Death Star Fat at twice the speed of light and there's no escape.

'Ian?'

I'm drowning. What can I do? I know, I'll make her laugh. She loves it when I'm funny.

I fold my arms, smile broadly and say, 'Hey, your bum always looks big. Just take the one with the bow.'

2

Tash's face is white. Her jaw has dropped.

How could I have said that!

I panic. 'No! I mean in an attractive way, it was a joke . . .'

Then, it happens.

Without realizing it, I gasp in air and the kebab goes down the wrong way. I choke and grab my throat. Tash is yelling at me. I really can't breathe. I need water, but I can't get off the couch because they'll see the stain.

Tash suddenly sees that I'm serious and starts hitting me on the back. The shop assistant runs up, still holding an armful of dresses wrapped in plastic. She dumps them on the couch and rushes off to get me some water. She's gone! Still wheezing, I jump to my feet and drag the dresses across the stain.

I might die, but at least they won't see that the couch is wrecked.

Tash thumps me so hard I lurch forward into a rack of wedding dresses just inside the door. It's on wheels. As I grab at it the whole thing goes careering out of the shop with me attached and crashes into a bunch of passing tourists. I fall and the rack crashes on top of me. I'm smothered in a mountain of plastic-covered wedding dresses. I'm gasping.

What a way to die.

No way. I fight my way up out through the dresses, still choking. The tourists are gathering round me. The shop assistant rushes up to help. I stagger to my feet, retch horribly – and a big lump of kebab flies out of my mouth and plops down on to her foot.

The crowd wails in disgust. I catch sight of Natasha's appalled face and yell, 'I couldn't help it!' as she storms off to get changed. Her last words as she crashes back into the cubicle and slashes the curtain shut are that not only do I vomit over people, but I've just said she's got a butt like a police horse.

As soon as Tash comes out of the cubicle she storms off into the packed crowds. I dash after her. Luckily our town is so full of tourists these days that the shop assistant will never recognize me again. Well, I hope not, since no way is that stain on the couch going to come out.

Why do these things always happen to me?

I catch up to Tash. She's pushing her way through a crowd of Japanese tourists that are being led by a man holding up a yellow umbrella. She's trying not to cry. I could kick myself.

'Please, Tashie. Let's talk. Look, Alana's coffee shop. They've got that cheesecake you like – let's go in there.'

ı, right. "Pack on a few more kilos while
ıe at it, big bum. No one will notice".'
Oh God, done it again.

'No, I didn't mean that, and you know I think you're
fantastic just the way you are. I think you're lovely.'

She stops. She's in tears now. 'Ian, that's not the
point. It's not what you think. It's what the world
thinks. I really want to look good at this concert. I don't
want to look like some big fat . . . sausage . . . packed
into a silk dress.'

'But you will look good. You're totally good-
looking.'

She's wavering. I'm frantic. I cast around for fash-
ion suggestions.

'I mean, can't you wear that . . . blue top thing?'

'What blue top thing?'

'The one you wear at the animal refuge. I really like
that.'

She's puzzled, then she sighs and breaks into a
despairing smile. 'Rudie . . .'

Aha. My pet name. I'm making a comeback. She
takes my hands.

'I can't go on stage in front of three hundred people
just wearing the T-shirt I put on to clean out the animal
pens.'

Silence.

I shrug. 'Well, if it *was* all you were wearing, you'd
bring the house down.'

She grins and whacks me with her ecologically

sound, non-plastic shopping bag. Tash, I should say, is seriously into saving the planet.

Alana's coffee shop is full of tourists, so we end up at an outside table in a grimy little Internet cafe called Tiger Video and DVD Rentorama and Internet Cafe. It used to be called Dink's Videos. It's run by an ex-truckie called Dinka who everyone in town knows sold his rig because of uncontrollable road rage. He changed the name to improve business. Unfortunately, it's not the name that's wrong, it's Dink. Dink has transferred his road rage to his customers. So the minute you go in he's turning purple and trying not to grab you by the collar and shake you because you don't know instantly what DVD or drink you want, or how much time you need on the Net.

Since we're awake to Dink, we order the second he comes over to our table. He writes it down with a stumpy pencil, breathing heavily. I get a cappuccino and a burger. Tash sips a black tea. She's forgiven me for puking on the basis that I would otherwise have choked to death. She's decided to go dress shopping some other time with one of her girlfriends instead. And she's going on a diet.

I say she looks like she's lost weight already.

This isn't because I think so (or care). It's because I read in a magazine at the hairdresser's that it's the only safe thing to say to girls who announce they're going on a diet. It works like a dream. Tash smiles and says she thought her jeans were getting a bit looser.

Close shave, amigo.

Luckily, my mates Pricey and Bogle turn up soon after, sit down with us, and order one cappuccino between them, so we get off the weight issue once and for all. I've known Bogle and Price since I moved here three years ago. Bogle's a genius with about as much common sense as a day-old panda. Price is the kindest kid you could meet but he's got even less common sense than a day-old panda (and keeps us all in stitches because of it). What with me attracting disasters like a magnet, we're natural allies (and are also banned from working together in chemistry after a series of nasty accidents).

Bogle leans across the table. 'Hey, Rude-Man. Did you really puke up over someone's wedding dress? Typical or what?'

Pricey chuckles. This is what our town's like. You can't breathe without someone up the other end of town sending a letter about it to the papers. I change the subject to *Cemetery Trashers III*. This is a safe bet because Bogle, who's a full-on geek and lives for computer games, is currently obsessed with it and will spend hours discussing tactics. Sure enough, he's off straight away, going on about the number of different reasons the game gives you for digging up corpses. Pricey gets totally confused and thinks someone's actually been digging up corpses somewhere locally. Since I can't stand *Cemetery Trashers*, I try getting a rise out of Bogle by saying how stupid I reckon it is.

But instead of reacting he suddenly hisses, 'Shh. Shut up, it's Ruby Pearson!'

Pricey's gone all pink. It's the weirdest thing. Pricey's way good-looking, but he's the shyest guy around girls I've ever seen. When one he likes gets within ten metres he goes brilliant red and sweats like he's attached to a hose. And he really likes Ruby Pearson, who at this minute is walking towards us up the shopping mall with her friend Kate.

Ruby and Kate are Folders.

You've seen Folders.

Folders are packs of super-cool girls who go around with their arms folded. All the time. Even when they're walking into assembly. Even when they're running for the bus. Even when they're eating they keep one arm clamped in the fold position. And it takes just one mention of The Folders to remind Pricey of Ruby, which then reminds him that he needs to mutate into Mr Strawberry-Head and sweat.

Natasha says, 'It's OK, Pricey. Just talk to her.'

Bogle says, 'Whoa, Price, you're fully scarlet. Open your mouth and people'll start posting letters in the slit.'

I cut in. 'Shut up, Bogle. Pricey, just stay calm and go for it.'

Ruby and Kate come up, in full folded position. They stop. Ruby looks straight at Price and says, 'Hi, guys. We're going to the movies. Anyone want to come?'

We all turn to him. He's burning red. You can actually feel the heat coming off his face. The sweat's broken out on his forehead.

Go, Pricey. This is the moment you've been waiting for.

Pricey gulps, sways, frantically taps his teaspoon on his coffee cup, gives a high-pitched laugh – and punches Bogle on the shoulder.

What?

Twin beads of sweat are running past his ears.

He shrieks hysterically. 'Hee-hee! Ya know, Bogle's inventing a self-opening toilet roll. *Ha!* Way dumb!' And drops his spoon.

It clatters in the appalled silence. As Pricey glances down, a big bead of sweat falls off the end of his chin and drops into his cappuccino with a 'plip'.

After an agonizing pause, Ruby and Kate look at each other. Ruby extracts a long, slim hand to slip a stray lock of hair behind her ear, then clamps back into full fold.

She smiles politely. 'Whadever. See you.'

She and Kate walk off, fully folded. A little way away they burst into smothered giggles, their shoulders shaking.

We're all open-mouthed. Pricey stares at us savagely. '*What?*'

He punches the seat, says the F word (the other one) and stalks off. Bogle goes after him to cheer him up. Poor old Price. Mind you, I don't know what he sees in The Folders. They're totally smug and self-obsessed. As far as I'm concerned, Price can keep 'em.

Natasha and I head off soon after. She's got to get organized for the youth orchestra music programme she's starting at this afternoon for the next couple of weeks, the one with the piano concert at the end that she needs the dress for. As we're leaving the shopping mall we see Price and Bogle. Pricey's frantically kicking the brick wall of the Supa Mart car park, while Bogle's yelling at him to snap out of it.

Tash stares at Pricey. 'Hmm. Unresolved sexual tension.'

I leer. 'That sounds interesting . . .'

She grins. 'In your dreams . . . ! Let's walk via the beach.'

We go along the beach front and buy a bag of chips. Just to tease her, I feed bits to the seagulls.

You see, Tash is a serious environmentalist. She reckons that feeding animals interferes with the natural order and the seagulls round here should be culled anyway because they wreck things for other seabirds.

She laughs and tries to grab the bag of chips. We wrestle, and she gets it off me at the very moment a really aggro, tatty old seagull with a wonky beak and only one leg hops up.

She waves the bag in the air – then gives him the lot. We laugh. We both know she's doing it because she feels sorry for him. But she tries to invent this big excuse about exterminating it by feeding it to death.

I say I plan to exterminate all the *perfect* gulls. This would leave only the one-legged, wonky-beaked ones with attitude. Which means I can then breed a master race of weird, vicious gulls that will end up pecking environmentalists like her to death. I act out the death-attack of the Giant Wonky-Beaks, doing squawking noises and pecking stabs at her with my fingers that tickle her till she's shrieking with laughter, fighting me off. The only way to stop the Giant Wonky-Beaks is to say, 'Ian is king.'

I take her in my arms. She smiles. 'Hey, Rudie. Sorry I was mean before. I just hate buying clothes. And you were being so nice.'

I narrow my eyes. 'This is because I am a hero among men.'

She gives me a lovely soft kiss and she's gone.

Ah, Tash.

3

Life is good. If only Tash wasn't going on this music programme thing it would be perfect. I was looking forward to being together during the holidays, just hanging out. Instead, she's spending two weeks with a bunch of musical geniuses from all over the world at St Joey's boarding school in the centre of Yarradindi, our town.

Still, that's the downside of going out with a girl who's some kind of musical genius. She plays a whole range of instruments, including the cello, which she's really good at. But – hey – it could have been worse. At least we'll be in the same town. Last year they had the music camp in Melbourne.

And let's face it, you can't have a beautiful, brilliant girlfriend and not expect her to have a life of her own. And she is beautiful and brilliant. When it comes to smarts, I'm just not in her league. To be honest, I spend a lot of the time wondering what she sees in me. It sure ain't my looks.

We're meeting up at St Joey's gates at one forty-five, towards the end of her lunch break. I head home to help in our family's shop in the meantime. Suddenly, I·hear a blast of cow mooing, but I know instantly it's not a cow. In fact, it's the hooter of a black four-seater ute with flames painted on the side, which screeches to a halt alongside me, revving throatily. It's got a new sign on the back saying: 'Pocky and Son, Home Repairs and Martial Arts Training', next to an old one which reads: 'Don't be a Jerk, give Pocky your Work'.

I hear a gargled roar. 'Wharrar puke all overa dress shop, a silly begga, aaah!' It's old Syd Pocky. He's leaning out of the passenger-side window. I should explain about the Pockys. The Pockys are this big local family. They're all skinny, blond, pointy-featured and psychopathic. Well, only the kids are psychopathic. The adults are quite nice. The adults are what my dad (one of life's optimists) calls 'enthusiasts'. This is code for being cheerfully mad with a tendency to violence. For example, take Syd Pocky, the grandad. Syd's little, wears black shorts and a navy blue singlet every day of the year (when he's not in his motorbike leathers) and is covered in tattoos. He and his wife, Granny Pocky, run the motorbike repair place next door to my family's health-food shop.

Granny's brilliant at fixing motorbikes. She's instantly recognizable by the crocodile tattooed in her cleavage.

Syd's instantly recognizable because of the noise he makes. I think years of listening to motorbike exhausts have made him a bit deaf. Whatever it is, he's constantly bellowing cheerfully at you and kind of gargling and slurring his words, so mostly what you hear is just the 'lucky beggas' he puts at the end of almost every sentence.

Terry, who's driving, is Syd and Granny's son. He's a martial arts teacher and the world's worst handyman. When he's not creating disasters with carpentry jobs that fall apart and plumbing fixtures that drop off walls, his hobbies are skydiving and stopping overhead fans by pressing his head hard up against the middle bit. He's got amazing long, shiny blond hair and, today, a T-shirt that reads: 'Don't be a doofus, let Pocky and Son be your roofers'. He's always had T-shirts with slogans like these, but now that his first son, Dylan, has left school to work with him, it's 'Pocky and Son'.

Dylan, sitting in the back, is a different matter. He used to go to our school, until he got apprenticed to Terry. He's making vicious faces at me as he cleans his nails with the end of a chisel. Syd gave him a leather tool belt to celebrate joining the family firm. He wears it constantly for general vandalism purposes.

And there are about two hundred more Pocky uncles, aunts, brothers, sisters, cousins, nephews and nieces who aren't present. The ones I know best are Clint, Dylan's younger brother, who's in my class at school and is famous for the unprovoked rabbit punch between the shoulders in the corridor, and Troy Pocky, Terry's youngest, who's one of the few pre-schoolers you'll ever meet who can give a kid twice his size a wedgie to make the eyes water. For the last couple of weeks they've been joined by their cousin Chett Pocky. Chett's just passed his driving test, so he spends entire weekends roaring around the shopping centre in an old blue Monaro with a broken exhaust, the stereo pumping.

I get to see a lot of the Pocky kids since they're always visiting next door to us, to see Syd and Granny Pocky. In fact, I'd have to say I see a lot more of the Pocky kids than I'd like to – and I've got the bruises to prove it.

Anyhow, life's really changed for all the Pockys recently. In fact, it's changed for the whole town, and all because of the Pockys. The point is, a couple of months ago, giant versions of a whole bunch of animal species that everyone thought were extinct were found living happily in the dense rainforest at the back of the Pockys' old farm. Wildlife experts and tourists have been flocking into town ever since.

The big attraction is the Yarradindi Tiger. This is our local version of the extinct Thylacine, or Tasmanian Tiger, but much bigger. It's a huge, ugly, stripy, wolf-like animal with a long, pointed snout. Everyone thought it had completely died out everywhere in Australia, until the Pockys revealed that their place had been infested with the tigers for as long as anyone could remember. In fact, the Pockys were amazed that anyone was interested in them, since they'd always seen them as a darn nuisance, getting into the garbage bins and nipping people and hanging round at barbies pinching the sausages.

They'd been using them for target practice for centuries.

You can imagine the effect on local tourism. The council paid a cartoonist to invent a smiling tiger character called 'Tyson, the Yarradindi Tiger'. Now every shop's stocking stuffed tigers or pictures of tigers or bottle openers with a tiger on top. There are queues everywhere for absolutely everything. People are renting out their rooms for B. & B. There are scientists everywhere, and film crews are always turning up to do documentaries. And at the Pockys' farm the crowds passing through to see the endangered species are amazing. The place is now called 'Yarradindi Australian Safari Park'. The Pockys have been selling souvenirs and refreshments. They're running walking tours and are even in the process of building special ecologically sound cabins with solar power and recycled water to attract eco-tourists to stay for the holiday they'll never forget. Given Terry's ability to build things that fall down or drop apart at the most unexpected moments, it probably will be the holiday they never forget. That's if they don't get concussed by falling bits of eco-cabin and lose their memory altogether.

The Pockys' other big money-spinner is Pockyloos. You've heard of Portaloos. Well, now that the town's full of tourists there's a shortage of public toilets, so Terry's invented a cheap version to cope with the demand. It's called, naturally, The Pockyloo. It's made of four second-hand doors joined together by hinges. Add a canvas flap on top for a roof and a camping toilet (which is just a big tin can with a dunny seat on top) inside, and that's it. There are heaps of them all folded and stacked in the back of the ute at this moment.

But Terry explains that today they're in town for Syd to pick up their new amphibian tour bus, The Tysonmobile. This was purchased by Crusher, Terry's brother, who used to be a commando and has connections in army disposals.

Today's the first tour. Terry beams with pride. 'Gonna take twenty tourists a time over the swamp right into tiger territory!'

Syd interrupts him. 'Norra *"swamp"*, a silly begga. Gorra call a *"Yarradindi Wetlands"*, aaaah!'

Terry chuckles. 'And you'd never guess, Ian mate – your dad'd have a laugh at this – we had a scientist up there last week – said it's fulla prehistoric fish! Fair dinkum! Just think, coupla months ago we was gonna concrete it over for a car park!'

Right now The Tysonmobile is at the sign painters having 'Yarradindi Australian Safari Park Tours' painted on the side. They're also putting a big cartoon picture of Tyson the Tiger's face on the bonnet of the bus with, as a joke, a picture of Tyson's backside on the bus's rear end.

Syd cuts in solemnly. 'But gorra be tail in down position, so norra rude.'

Terry gives a hoot of laughter. 'Too right – you wouldn't want to be driving up the freeway for hours face-to-face with Tyson's big hairy danglies.'

'Gerra move on, Terry, a pickin' up a tourists, a lucky beggas . . .'

Terry revs the ute. 'Right you are, Dad. See ya, Ian. And remember: if you or your mates are ever stuck for cash, there's always a heap a jobs up at the safari park. Ten bucks an hour and all the food you can eat.'

Behind him, Dylan writhes his mouth and jabs his chisel upwards to show what me and my mates will get if we even think about coming near his safari park.

I say, 'Thanks, Mr Pocky,' and make a mental note never to have anything to do with the place. Not only because of Dylan, but because working for Terry means I'll probably end up losing a leg or an arm.

Terry grins and pumps the cow hooter as he guns the ute up the road. In the back, his speckled cattle dog, Ripperson (son of Syd's dog, Ripper), barks frantically.

As always after the Pockys have left, it's strangely quiet.

I try to stay clear of the Pockys these days for another reason apart from physical safety. Natasha.

Along with her mum and dad, Mr and Mrs Frye,

Tash lives in a little house set in paddocks just down the hill from the Pockys' farm. Living next door to the Pockys would be trouble for anyone, but since Natasha and both her parents are all full-on environmentalists, it's a nightmare. The problem is that while the Pockys are sitting on the most important wildlife discovery of the twenty-first century, they've never really got it that they're supposed to protect it. They just see it as another great business opportunity.

So they've been happily packing in as many tourists as possible and trying to add attractions like skydiving into the rainforest and waterskiing on the wetlands. The council knocked those back, but the Fryes were outraged at the very thought. Mr Frye, who up to then had been running the walking tours for the Pockys, went bananas and resigned. He's now trying to make a living by showing people round his eco-friendly cottage and ramshackle wildlife refuge. Unfortunately the tourists aren't turning up. So he spends most of his time stomping around his animal pens, raving on about how the government should clamp down on the Pockys, confiscate their land and throw the lot of them in jail.

Meanwhile Mrs Frye, Natasha's mum, is away a lot, travelling the world as a bat expert, so that leaves just Tash and her psycho dad most of the time. All in all, things are pretty tense at Tash's place because of the Pockys. It's amazing that Tash is as sane as she is, really.

I get home to find our cafe packed with tourists. People are massing at the counter to get their Tiger burgers, which are made of tofu, mayo and tomato, with three lines of brown sauce on top to represent stripes. We run a health-food shop and cafe called (since our surname's Rude) Rude Health. This was my dad's idea. Dad's motto is 'Think Positive'. He reckons we should open a shop selling speakers and music gear and call it (yes) 'Rude Sound'.

The fact that the Year 10 mafia would beat me to a pulp seems to have escaped him.

'Hi, Ian.' It's Mum. 'Can you get Dad in from the porch to help?'

In the middle of saying this, she jumps up to a shelf, snatches a bottle of tomato sauce and lands again without missing a beat. She needs to jump because she's so small. All my family are small. We learn to jump for things from an early age, but it amazes people when they see it for the first time. What really gets them is the way we continue the conversation in mid-air.

I head out to the porch, which is a tatty, covered-in space at the back of the house. Suddenly, there's the most amazing ripping sound, followed by wild laughter from my two-year-old sister, Daisy. As I turn the corner Dad's head bobs up from behind two towers of cardboard boxes. He's got a hammer in one hand and a big lump of ancient lino in the other.

He grins. 'G'day, mate. Welcome to "The Garden Room".'

'The what?'

'The new extension to the cafe. We'll rip up the lino, polish the boards – hey presto.'

Not another one of Dad's projects.

4

'Grab that bit.'

Dad hooks the claw end of the hammer under a loose flap of lino. I grab a corner that's already sticking up. He wrenches and I tear. A great big chunk of lino rips up with an amazing barking sound.

'Steve?'

It's Mum, freaked.

'Why are you destroying the lino? I've got a cafe full of people out there.'

'Precisely. When I've polished up the floorboards we can fit another twenty in here.'

Daisy's got a scrap of lino on her head as if it's a hat.

'Steve, not in the middle of the lunchtime rush . . .'

'It'll only take a few hours. In two days we'll be packing them in. Tell you what.' He turns to me. 'Ian can rip up the lino while I go back to the shop with you. After he's done that I can do the sanding and varnishing. How about it, mate? Three dollars an hour.'

Mum tuts irritably. 'Ian can't do it – Daisy, take that

off your head – this is a huge job, Steve. And where are we going to put those piles of boxes?'

I interrupt. 'I *can* do it.'

I quite like the idea of all that ripping. Plus the money's always handy.

Dad puts his hands on his hips and grins. 'Well, I've started it now. We can't leave it like this, can we?'

Mum sighs. She knows Dad well enough to realize that once he's started something there's no stopping him. This is why we ended up in Yarradindi in the first place – Dad got made redundant and instantly decided we all needed to leave the city and live on the coast.

Also, of course, the porch is now completely wrecked.

Mum jumps up to a shelf and snatches a pair of gardening gloves for me. Dad scoops up Daisy, and the three of them head back into the shop. I set to, ripping. Unfortunately, I soon find out that it's only the lino in the middle of the floor that comes up easily. The rest of it's stuck fast with some kind of thick, black, tar-like glue. I find Dad to tell him. He's unfazed.

'Not to worry. I'll borrow a proper scraper from the Pockys and finish it later. Here.'

He winks and gives me four bucks. This is our secret. Mum reckons I should help the family for nothing, out of family duty. Dad reckons I should get paid at least five dollars an hour. They've agreed to give me three for bigger jobs, but Dad's always slipping me an extra dollar on the side. Morally, I agree with Mum, but I have to say, the cash never goes amiss.

Just then my mobile rings. It's Tash. She wants me to pick up her cello from the man who's repairing it. Her dad was supposed to do it, but he's tied up with a sick wombat.

I head off. The repairer lives at 25 Long Street. Someone's changed the sign to Pong Street.

Number 25 is dark and overgrown. There's a brass plaque next to the front door: 'Simon Pilple, violin maker and stringed-instrument repair'. The door's opened by a skinny, miserable-looking man. I guess this is Simon. He's dressed completely in brown. The house smells weirdly of cabbages and something sweet.

'I've come to pick up Natasha Frye's cello.'

'Who are you, her brother?'

'Boyfriend.'

Pilple grunts, stares into the distance and mutters, 'I used to trust women.' He blinks. 'It was a mistake.'

Terrific. This town is full of loons. It must be the sea air.

The cello is in a big black case with little wheels on the bottom so you can pull it along behind you like a suitcase. I rattle off down the street.

The case is pretty cool. It'd be a great place to stash a corpse if you had to take one anywhere. A pretty small corpse. Although maybe you could squeeze in a bigger one if you rolled it up before rigor mortis set in.

It occurs to me that I'm really happy. It always happens when I'm due to see Tash.

As I get closer to the shopping centre, Pricey and Bogle appear from an alleyway. They're still arguing, which is standard after Pricey's made an idiot of himself. Next, Pricey will get Bogle in a headlock. There he goes. They come staggering down the street, Pricey dragging Bogle by the head, Bogle punching him.

'Yo, Rudie! What you doing with a cello?'

This is Bogle, from his headlock.

I say, 'It's Tash's. Let him go, Price, his eyes are bulging.'

Pricey gives Bogle's head another wrench, then frees it.

Bogle looks up cheerfully and adjusts his glasses. 'Hey, Price, how about going to the supermarket?'

'Get nicked, you wacko.'

Bogle wants to go to the supermarket to indulge in his favourite (and seriously weird) hobby of squeezing plastic-wrapped meat, particularly the squashy bits.

Bogle's going, 'Oh come on, Price . . .' He stops because someone's leaning on the horn of a car and voices are yelling.

It's Chett Pocky in his beaten-up Monaro. A whole bunch of Pockys, including Clint and his fat mate Cunningham, are in the back. They're bellowing insults at us.

Since we're at a safe distance, we yell more back. Especially Pricey. He's really getting into it, I s'pose because he's still furious with himself about Ruby.

As the Pockys drive past, Price starts up a rhyme that we used to sing about them at school (as revenge for things like getting your underpants chucked on the changing-room roof after swimming). 'All Pockys are dumb. Faces like my bum.' It's so moronic, it's funny.

On the second line I can't stop laughing. Soon all three of us are chanting it, plus doing the traditional pointing at our butts. Bogle stares after the Monaro as it screeches off around the corner.

He drawls, 'Ratbags!' and we stroll on in the sudden silence.

There's a squeal of tyres. The Monaro comes reversing back round the corner with Chett honking the horn wildly and the Pocky kids hanging out of the window, whooping and yelling.

How could I have forgotten the effect that rhyme has on the Pocky kids?

The Monaro screeches to a halt and about ten Pockys, plus Cunningham, jump out yelling, 'Get 'em!'

'Run for it!'

We belt off down the street. I'm running as fast as I can, but the cello's slowing me down. I'll never get away. It's rocking and swaying on its wheels and smacking into lamp posts.

Clint and Dylan are gaining on me. Ahead, Pricey and Bogle leap over a low wall and head down an alleyway. I can't follow them because of the cello. Most of the Pockys follow Pricey and Bogle. Clint and Cunningham follow me.

I'm in a dead end. The only way out is down the ramp into an underground car park. I pelt down. But the cello tries to overtake me. It thumps into the backs of my ankles. I stagger. It bumps into my ankles again. I'm gone. I hit the ground and roll. The cello goes bouncing and skidding along the ground. And Clint and Cunningham are on top of me, thumping and yelling.

Like an idiot, I shout, 'Mind the cello!'

I could bite off my tongue. Clint and Cunningham instantly lose interest in me and start fighting for the cello. Cunningham grabs it and starts swinging it around.

'Hoo-hoo, Rudie wants his guitar!'

'Give it back, it's really valuable!'

'Big girl wants his guitar!'

'Give it back, you dork!'

'You want it, get it!'

He runs off round the car park, holding it over his head. Then he swings it back down to earth and jumps astride it like it's a hobby horse. Clint's shrieking like a chimp. I'm bellowing at them to stop.

Clint yells, 'Gimme a go!'

He grabs the case, shoves it in front of him at high

speed, then lets go. I gasp. The cello whizzes and bounces along the ground. I throw myself after it, but Cunningham grabs it first. My voice cracks, I'm shouting so loud.

At that moment there's an engine roar, a scream of tyres and tooting. It's Chett in the Monaro, with the rest of the Pockys, all killing themselves laughing.

Chett yells, 'Get in! Get in! It's old Platt!'

Thank God. I can hear Constable Platt's police siren from here. I lunge for the cello again. But now Clint's got it. They pile with it into the back of the Monaro and roar off. I run after them, yelling in horror. At the same moment Pricey and Bogle come thundering in the side entrance of the car park.

'Rudie, you OK?'

'They got the cello!'

Bogle starts running. 'We gotta see where they take it. They'll have to go across High Street.'

He's right. It's the only way they can get out of the one-way system. We shoot off through the back way and come out at the end of High Street – just as the Monaro swerves into sight around the corner. I can see the cello crammed in the back on top of a mob of Pockys. Pricey bellows, 'The one-way system'll take 'em to the freeway. We can cut them off at Tate Street.'

How could I have let this happen? We speed through the pedestrian mall. Now we've got to cross a busy intersection to get to Tate Street. A giant truck roars past with a gust of wind. How are we going to stop the Pockys? How are we even going to get across this road?

There's a brief gap in the traffic. We fly across, race down an alleyway and come out on Tate Street just as the Monaro is roaring towards us. Now what? Run out in front of it? There's six lanes of traffic. But Bogle's pelting to the pedestrian island. Price and me join him. It's hardly an island. It's more like a bit of concrete in the middle of a stock-car race track. I'm shaking my fist helplessly and shouting.

Chett slams on his brakes. All the cars behind him squeal to a halt. The Monaro's back door opens and the cello case comes hurtling out as Chett accelerates and roars off. The case lands heavily, bounces, flies open – and the cello falls out, right in the middle of the road.

36

5

As we watch, a container truck clips one side of the cello. A ute hits the other. For what seems like forever, the cello and the case are in the middle of the road being knocked to and fro by trucks and cars. I feel sick.

Finally, there's a gap in the traffic. We dart out onto the road, grab the cello and its case and struggle back with them to the pavement.

Bogle's aghast. 'Is it OK?'

I'm choked. The case is OK, but the cello is a wreck. The neck's snapped so the strings are dangling. The bridge has gone. Bits of wood have been chipped off its sides. The only thing that's intact is the bow. I slump to the ground. Pricey bangs his forehead with his fist. 'I'm so sorry, man! If I hadn't mouthed off at the Pockys . . .'

He trails off. I shake my head. It's tempting to blame him, but all three of us were as bad as each other.

I gulp. 'D'you reckon we can fix it?'

Pricey's frantic. 'Let's buy a new one. How much are they?'

Bogle shrugs. 'It might be worth hundreds of thousands of dollars.'

'You're kidding.'

The look on his face tells me he's not.

I gulp. 'I guess we'd better take it back to Pilple and ask him how much to fix it.'

We rush to Pilple's, stopping at a cash machine to get out our savings. Between us we've got ninety dollars. Terrific.

Pilple takes one look at the cello and gasps like we've just committed a murder and we're showing him the body. He gently lifts the cello from me and puts it on a table, inspecting it.

I can't stand the suspense. 'How much to fix it today?'

His head jerks up. 'Today?' he snarls. 'Are you completely stupid? One thousand five hundred dollars, including parts. Alternatively, for a new cello of this quality, about two thousand. Repairs will take *three* days, minimum. And I don't start work until I'm paid in full.'

Pricey, Bogle and I stare at each other, horrified. What can we do? I try telling Pilple how much Tash needs her cello now. I tell him about the music camp. We say we'll get jobs or a loan. He says to ask our parents, we explain there's absolutely no way. Finally, he agrees irritably to take the ninety dollars as a deposit. He'll start on the cello when we've paid off half of the whole fee, seven hundred and fifty dollars. But only then. The full fee's got to be paid off in two weeks, in nightly instalments. And we don't get the cello until the final dollar is paid. 'Do you boys understand?'

We nod dumbly.

We can't get out of there fast enough.

I feel sick because I know I've got to ring Natasha and tell her. She'll be waiting at Joey's for me. What am I going to say? I punch in her number, top of my list. Bogle and Pricey stare at me as it rings.

'Hello, Ian? Where are you? You're late.'

'Tash. Look. Something's happened . . .'

This is agony.

'Ian? You're breaking up.'

'Your cello.' I gulp. 'We were at the shopping mall . . .'

'You're breaking up again.'

I yell. 'Your cello! It fell into the road and got broken. But don't worry, we're getting it fixed, the neck and everything.'

'You had a problem with the neck?'

'But the bow's fine.' I blurt, 'Tash, I feel terrible. How can you ever forgive me . . . ?'

There's silence. Then, I can't believe this, she's chuckling. 'Why wouldn't I forgive you?'

'You're not upset?'

This girl is amazing.

'Course not. I'll just get a different one. Don't be silly.'

'But you trusted me.'

'Forget it. Come over to Joey's now and meet everyone.'

As I hang up, Bogle and Pricey are looking at me.
'What did she say?'

I'm in a state of shock. 'She's fantastic. She
laughed. She said it didn't matter.'

Pricey's wide-eyed. 'You're so lucky, man. I acci-
dentally blew out one of my parents' speakers once and
they went ballistic.'

I'm glowing with relief. Natasha. She is so gorgeous. No matter what she says, I'm going to pay for
repairs. I'll fix everything. I'll find a job and keep
doing the lino for Dad. I'll sell my stuff. Price and
Bogle will help. As we set off to see her I'm brimming
with gratitude.

She's standing outside the gates of St Joey's looking lovely.

'Tash, I am *so* sorry.'

'Don't be silly. Why would you think I'd be upset?
Hi, Bogle. Hi, Pricey.'

'I so stuffed up. I mean, dumb *as* . . .'

She leads me off round the corner for privacy. 'Now
stop it. I don't care. It's all forgotten. It wasn't fair to
ask you in the first place.'

'But you were trusting me. You gave me all that
responsibility and I let you down.'

She grins. 'You're so cute to worry like this.'

I feel another huge wave of relief. 'The bow's fine.
It's the neck that's really the problem . . .'

She smiles more. 'Oh look, I never liked that neck. The neck on the blue one was much better.'

A blue cello? I'm surprised. 'I didn't know they made them in blue.'

She punches me and laughs. 'Stop winding me up. You've been talking about the blue one. You liked it. It was short.' She leans towards me thoughtfully. 'That's the thing. D'you think I should go for a short one? I mean, I liked the blue one but, well, it was so close-fitting . . .'

Close-fitting?

She frowns anxiously and takes my hand. 'Now, this is a serious question, so don't joke.' She leans forward and murmurs, 'Do you think it's a bit see-through?'

Something is terribly wrong. Why is she talking about short blue cellos? And see-through cellos? I feel a cold wave of panic.

'And Ian? I know you like the neck and the bow on the blue one, but at the back of my mind I'm wondering whether I'm buying it just for the label. I mean, you don't have to buy a *designer* dress to look good.'

It suddenly dawns. *We're talking about dresses.*

'Incidentally, can you still pick up the cello, or shall I get Dad to do it?'

6

This is a bad dream. This is insane. I've just told Tash I've smashed up her cello but she thinks I'm talking about dresses. She smiles. 'Because I can ring him and ask him to pick it up. It's just that he's so busy with the animals.'

I stutter, 'No, no, I'll do it,'

How can this have happened? I told her everything. It must have been my phone cutting out. She must have heard me saying something about the bow and the neck and thought I was talking about dresses. I have to tell her all over again.

She beams. 'I can't believe you got worried about not liking some dress.'

I'm standing in silence, stupefied.

She grabs my arm and gasps, 'Hey, guess what Günter, one of the German exchange students, was telling me. This terrible story. Apparently, some boy he knows asked his brother to pick his cello up from the repair shop, and the stupid dork dropped it so *it got this huge crack in it*!'

I croak.

She nods. 'Yeah, isn't it terrible! Can you imagine anything worse?'

Like, it ending up smashed to bits by three lanes of traffic? What am I going to do? Just then a big door in the hall behind us opens and a good-looking blond guy comes out. A bit too good-looking.

Natasha introduces him as Günter. I put my arm round her, just so he gets the picture. She turns to me. 'I've got to go. See you at seven after rehearsal.' She stops. 'And Ian – you worrying about my dress. You are SO CUTE.'

I smile weakly.

I am gone. Finished. Wipe-out. I wave as she disappears through the gates, then stagger back to Pricey and Bogle and fill them in.

'I can't possibly tell her now.'

Bogle snorts. 'You've got to.'

'Get real, man. She loves that cello. When she finds out what I've done she'll never want to see me again.' I stop. Something occurs to me. 'That's *if* she finds out what I've done.'

Bogle stares at me. 'You mean, fix it and not tell her?'

Pricey chuckles. 'That's so cool. Wish I'd done that with my parents' speakers . . .'

'No, I mean, tell her *after* it's fixed. When there's nothing to get upset about.'

'That's insane. Pilple'll tell her.'

I'm stoked. This is brilliant. 'Why *should* he tell her? What's it to him?'

'But we can't hold her off for two weeks.'

'We don't have to. Pilple said he could do it in three days.'

Bogle snorts with frustration. 'From when he started, which is when he's got half the money . . .'

I'm already ringing Pilple. 'Yeah, dur-brain, so that's why we gotta start earning the money.'

'Man, you've lost it, you can't trust that whacko . . .'

'Listen to me. She's tied up at this music camp. All I've got to do is get Pilple to keep his mouth shut, which —'

Pilple picks up.

'Mr Pilple, it's Ian Rude. Me and my friends just came to see you about fixing my girlfriend's cello . . .'

The best I can get out of him is that he won't actively contact anyone in the Frye family about what's going on, but if someone asks, he'll have to tell the truth. I hang up.

'*Yes!*'

Bogle folds his arms. 'You are one total prize walking disaster, Rude . . .'

'Trust me, it'll work.'

'What if our parents find out?'

'They won't. Are you in this or not?'

'Course I'm in it. I just want you to be reasonable.'

But I'm ignoring him. Right. Action.

As I stride down the road he's nagging me like an old granny while Price is jogging alongside, talking about his parents' speakers. I'm sending a broadcast text to everyone I know, offering to sell my CDs and my skateboard. (My skateboard! That hurts. That really hurts.) The next thing is to find a job. I veer off towards the shopping centre.

Bogle throws up his hands. 'Where you going now?'

'To get jobs, dork-head. We haven't got time to waste.'

'Why are you going to the shops? The place for jobs is the Pockys'.'

'The Pockys'? You're kidding. That disaster zone.'

Price butts in. 'He's right, man. There are heaps of jobs going at the Pockys'. They've got posters up all over town.'

'I'm not hanging around the Pockys' ready for Mr Frye to see me and tell Tash. It's bad enough she might find out I broke the cello. If she found out I was working for the Pockys, she'd go berserk.'

Bogle stops in his tracks. 'This gets more stupid by the minute. The only fast way we can raise the kind of money we're after is by working for the Pockys. No one else pays ten dollars an hour!'

We start arguing. I suggest we get shop jobs and clean car windows at the traffic lights. Bogle says the council's banned car window cleaning and reckons all the jobs for people our age are already taken, apart from up at the Pockys', because it's the holidays. Price wants to ask his dad for a loan. I say he can't because the first thing his dad'll do is tell my dad, which means the news will get straight back to Mr Frye.

Bogle is yelling, 'The longer this goes on the more likely we'll get caught out.'

Price is yelling, 'Let me get a loan from my dad.'

I'm starting to panic. Time is ticking away. How can I work at the Pockys' with Mr Frye lurking about in the paddocks next door?

My phone rings. It's Tash.

Oh no!

I'm super-cheerful. My voice comes out strangely high. 'Hello there!'

'Hi. Have you picked up the cello yet?'

'Funny you should say that.' I gulp. 'Pilple, he's, er . . . gone.'

'Gone? Gone where?'

'Away for a few days.'

'But I was only talking to him this morning.'

'I know!' I gush. 'Just . . . weird, isn't it?'

'He can't just go away. When's he coming back? I've got to have my cello. I'm playing on one loaned from school. It sounds like a dying cat.'

There's no way out but lying. As Bogle and Price stand there looking disapproving, I tell her I talked to a neighbour who said Pilple's back later this week. She's bewildered. I offer to keep on top of it. Luckily she has to go back to the rehearsal, so I'm off the hook. I hang up, sweating.

Bogle says, 'You are SO dumb.'

'Thanks, Bogle. I appreciate that helpful and useful comment. Why don't you stick your head in a brick wall?'

'*You* stick *your* head in a brick wall, doofus.'

It's back into a full-scale row.

Suddenly, from out of nowhere there's a two-tone blasting horn and an engine so loud it sounds like an aircraft is taxiing down the main street. Then, lurching round the corner comes the weirdest vehicle I've ever seen. People are stopping their cars in amazement to look. It's bright yellow and really tall. It's a cross between a giant Humvee, a tank, an open-topped bus and a boat. It's on tyres nearly the size of the ones you see on tractors, and with about the same sort of tread. It might have started life in the army, but now it's got about twenty alarmed-looking tourists on the top deck, wearing harnesses like you get in fighter planes and clutching on for dear life. A big cartoon Tasmanian Tiger's head grins down from the front.

It is, of course, The Tysonmobile.

7

Syd's high up at the enormous steering wheel, located under Tyson's head. Presumably, Tyson's backside (tail down) is on show at the back. Syd sees us and slams on the brakes. He's beaming at me, dressed in his special Yarradindi Australian Safari Park uniform of khaki shirt and jacket, plus a big hat with dangling corks. The engine's thrumming is so loud he has to bellow even louder than usual.

'Aaaah, relieve a see ya, a cheeky beggas, soma wronga tourists, don't unnerstanna a word. Watchasilly beggas!' He turns round and yells, 'Onna right a supermarket, big begga, a speciality a barbecue chook a wide range a frozen goods, lefta Federation Bandstand an Communidy Centera a build a council nineteen seventy-three, a use a three thousanna two hunnera twenny-three bricks, aaaaah!'

The tourists stare at him blankly.

An American voice says, 'Whaddid he say?'

Syd turns to us. 'Come aboard a translayda cleva beggas. Ten dollars an hour, alla food, beera tour guide?'

We look at each other. I think of the cello. I think of what Tash'll do to me if she finds out I work at the Pockys' – and of what Dylan, Chett and the rest of the Pocky kids will do to me when I get there. What choice do I have?

I look up at Syd. 'Mr Pocky, can we get our money at the end of every day?'

'Coursa! Come aborra, a silly beggas.'

Bogle and Pricey beam. Syd flips a switch and lowers a flight of steps. We swing ourselves up and clip ourselves into the harnesses. I turn to the tourists and translate what Syd said, adding, after the bit about the bricks, 'It was built by Mr Terry Pocky, a leading local builder and son of your driver here, Mr Sydney Pocky.'

The tourists smile and nod. Syd gargles with pleasure.

I don't mention the fact that the council is trying to sue Terry because the ceiling leaks and a giant crack has appeared right down one wall of the Baby Health Centre.

By now, Syd's rammed The Tysonmobile into gear and we lurch off, engine roaring. I look at Price and Bogle and shrug.

We pass a motel with a big sign saying: 'Experience our enormous spa!' Someone's graffitied it so it reads: 'Experience our enormous bra!' We hit a bump and the whole vehicle rocks to one side, then rights itself.

Various passengers scream since their seats aren't properly bolted in.

Between translations, I get the others into a huddle.

I kick off. 'OK, the main thing is to get Pilple started on the cello as soon as possible.'

Bogle agrees. 'So we all sell our stuff. There's a problem because Price and me have got to be home by about seven tonight, but if we both work here four hours today and you work, say, six, that's one hundred and forty dollars already, plus the ninety-dollar deposit towards the seven hundred and fifty we need before Pilple will start.'

I'm counting on my fingers. 'It's Tuesday today—'

Bogle interrupts. 'If Price and me work eight hours each tomorrow and you do twelve hours, that's two hundred and eighty dollars added to the two hundred and thirty, so, with the extra money from selling stuff and you working for your dad, we should have the deposit money by tomorrow night, or Thursday latest.'

'Cool!'

'After that, if we make two hundred and eighty bucks on Thursday and Friday working at the Pockys' and get another hundred and ninety from somewhere, say, selling more stuff, and you doing the lino for your dad, we can just do it, taking the cello back on Saturday or Sunday, whenever it's finished.'

There's a sudden squeal of brakes. We shoot forward in our seats and get grabbed back at the last minute by the harnesses. The Tysonmobile is at the bottom of the big hill that leads up to the Pockys' place – at the back of an enormous traffic jam.

Bogle raises an eyebrow. 'Five minutes working for the Pockys and we're in a road accident.'

Syd jumps down to investigate the hold-up. We follow, keeping an eye out for old Frye. Luckily, there's no sign of him. Right in the middle of the road is what looks like a giant corrugated baked-bean can the size of a caravan. In front of it is Terry's ute. Terry, with Dylan, is squatting down at the roadside, puzzling over two ragged bits of rope. A mob of angry drivers is standing round yelling at him. It's a water tank and it's obviously fallen off the tray of the ute. Nobody can work out how to get it back on again. How Terry ever got it on there in the first place is a mystery.

From behind me a cheery woman's voice says, '*Hel*-lo, boys. Looks as if there's some kind of problem.'

It's Mrs McClaren, leading about ten Japanese kids in school uniform through the crowd. Mrs McClaren used to be mayor. She's the mother of a girl at my school. She's nice enough, except she's always trying to educate you and she's big on charity work. You get the feeling she actually likes it when things go wrong because it means she'll have a chance to fix them.

Now she says, 'Say hello to our Japanese exchange students from Tokyo, Ian,' and adds loudly, 'This is a fine pickle!'

She then says something in Japanese, turns to me

and whispers, 'I've just said, "This is a fine pickle," in Japanese, explaining that to us it means, "Here is a serious problem." The point is –' she beams – 'a favourite side dish in Japanese cooking is pickled ginger, so I have linked the lesson to their own culture.'

She turns to the kids and shouts, 'A FINE PICKLE.'

They politely repeat, 'Fie pickow,' and laugh with a kind of desperate hysteria. They've obviously got no idea what she's talking about.

Mrs McClaren asks me if I ever considered the fact that in English 'quite good' means 'pretty good', but 'quite perfect' means 'completely perfect'.

I resist the urge to punch her in the head.

Ahead, Syd bellows to Terry, 'Warra trouble?' He points to Bogle, Price and me and adds, 'Ianna friends come aworkarus a cheeky beggas, aaah . . .'

Terry smiles briefly, then holds up the frayed rope, frowning. 'Darn imported rubbish. Dunno how I'm ever gonna get this begga up the hill.'

'Mr Pocky.' It's Mrs McClaren. 'May I suggest – you roll it up the hill like a log?'

Syd claps her on the back. 'Aaah! Staring us inna face, a silly beggas!'

Terry yells, 'Good on the old mayor!' Then adds, 'That's to say, *last* mayor, not old horse, Mrs Mac. No offence.'

'None taken, Mr Pocky.'

Mrs McClaren organizes us into teams and calls out, 'On the count of three. One, two, three!'

And everyone shoves like mad. The tank starts to roll slowly upwards. Mrs McClaren says she feels like an Ancient Egyptian because the Ancient Egyptians moved the stones for their pyramids by putting them on logs and rolling the logs along. Terry says he prob'ly smells like an Ancient Egyptian, he's sweating that much. Dylan gives me the finger. The top of the hill looms up, scattered with caravans and tents that house the scientists researching the new animals.

There's a wild yell in the distance. A tent's collapsed on a scientist. A mob of primary-age Pockys goes belting off. Troy's filming it on his mobile.

We go up past the old sheds, the new toilet block (plus a line of Pockyloos) and the Tiger Museum, which used to be the Emu Museum when the Pockys were running an emu farm. They still have one emu, Bruce Willis, called after that famous Australian actor Bruce Willis. (I know Bruce Willis is American, but try telling Syd that.) Right now, Bruce is in his enclosure looking wistfully into the one eye of his best mate, Noddy, the kangaroo. Noddy is ferocious and steals people's sandwiches.

Since everyone at the Pockys' is ferocious and steals people's sandwiches, he fits right in.

Tash has told me about the Tiger Museum. Apparently, it's got all the old emu stuff inside, plus photos of tigers and (this is where Tash starts to froth at the mouth with rage) things like tiger-skin rugs and hats, made by the Pockys when they were convinced the tigers were just annoying wild dogs that made a nuisance of themselves at the barbie.

At last we make it to the top of the ridge, near the car park, shop and cafeteria (which is the front bit of the old Pocky farmhouse, converted).

We stop, puffing. The view's fantastic because the land drops away sharply in front of us. Down the hill to one side is the Pocky swamp and rainforest, which is home to all the endangered species. On the other side, immediately in front of us about a hundred metres down the hill, is the Fryes' house, with Mr Frye's beautifully laid-out vegetable garden.

A sign reads: 'Welcome to Sun Cottage. We are eco-aware'.

And there he is, Mr Frye. Off in the distance, on the hill below his house at his sheds. That's good, he won't see us. Syd and the motorists dust off their hands and head down the hill, while Mrs McClaren tells the Japanese students the Latin names of all the trees. Dylan starts carving his name in one of them.

Meanwhile, Terry's leaning on the tank, smiling thoughtfully. He grins and says, 'Look at that view. Reminds me of the old days. Used to have a barbie down there on the other side of the swamp every Sunday, all the family. Sossies, sing-alongs. The kids trynna dunk old Great-Gran Hilda.' He sighs nostalgically. 'It's at times like these, boys, you know why ya live in the country.'

He gives the tank a friendly thump.

It starts to roll down the hill. Straight towards Natasha's place.

8

We all gasp. Terry yells and starts running after the tank, but it's gathering speed. Way down the hill Mr Frye's bellowing and shaking his fist.

Terry shouts, 'She'll be right, the fence'll stop it!'

At that moment the tank crashes straight through the Fryes' fence and sends a bunch of chooks flying madly up into the air, squawking. It flattens Mr Frye's vegetable garden, smacks heavily against the side of the house, bounces a metre in the air, lands and stops. There's a stunned silence.

A chook fluttering overhead lands on top of the tank, squawks and ruffles its feathers. One of the Japanese kids says solemnly, 'Fie pickow.'

Down in the valley, Mr Frye's going berserk. A volley of abuse floats up to us on the wind.

Terry's the first to speak.

'Look at that house. Still standing. Now that's Australian craftsmanship.'

Oddly, Mr Frye doesn't seem to see the positive side. He's powering up the hill, making a noise like a cross between an angry gorilla and a cappuccino machine. Mrs McClaren is already hurrying towards him to negotiate a peace settlement.

Bogle mutters, 'We're out of here. If Frye sees you working for the Pockys, you're cactus.'

Price stands staring thoughtfully at Frye shaking his fists. 'Y'know Mr Frye? D'you reckon he's a bit annoyed?'

I grab Price and drag him off. As we scuttle across to the main building, Crusher, Terry's brother, appears from the cafe. This is a bit of luck, since he can give us a job and get us out of the way in case Frye decides to storm up into the Pockys' place. We quickly explain that we're working for the Safari Park. Crusher folds his gigantic arms, ponders, then tells us to go round to the back of the cafe and help in the kitchen.

I only know three things about Crusher. The first is that he was a commando in the army, and before that, a cook. The second is that he knows about twenty different ways to kill you (not counting pressure points). The third is that he's excellent at making curtains, but we're not supposed to mention it.

We go round the back of the cafe.

I turn to the others. 'Watch out for Clint.'

This is just the sort of moment for Clint Pocky to jump out from behind the kitchen door and chop the nearest one of us in the neck. We peer in cautiously, but – excellent – there's no sign of Clint or any of the Pocky kids at all. Instead, about thirty adult Pockys are squeezed inside, all yelling cheerfully to each other. A skinny old man who looks like an even thinner version of Syd flips hamburger patties up in the air. When they land back on the hotplate, everyone yells and cheers.

Granny's there. 'G'day, boys! Yous working for us now? Wacko! Grab a knife, and I'll get some bread for you to start buttering!'

The man at the hotplate flicks another hamburger high in the air. It lands on the floor. Everyone roars with laughter. He scoops it back up and whacks it on the griddle. Everyone cheers.

Bogle mutters, 'Over there.'

He's pointing at Chett Pocky, who's in a corner, dressed in an apron and a chef's hat, stirring something in a bowl.

I'd forgotten – he's apprenticed to Crusher. At that moment Chett turns, sees us and snarls, 'How's your guitar, ya big girl . . . ?' He's just about to bop Bogle with his wooden spoon when Granny comes back carting a plastic crate full of sandwich bread. She tosses me a loaf. The croc in her cleavage rolls in the wrinkles.

'Just butter and stack 'em, boys. Chett'll put on the filling, soon as he's finished his fairy cakes.'

Chett looks at us, silently daring us to say something. I have a quick image of him battering me with a rolling pin in some corner behind a shed.

I text Mum that I won't be home until late, then set to, buttering the bread. My mind goes back to Tash and the cello. I know the odds are stacked against me, but all I've got to do is keep her in the dark for a few days. If she had normal parents, they'd investigate like a shot. But my luck's in with Mr Frye. He's a complete fruit loop. On the other side of the table Bogle and Price are buttering as well. Bogle's got a system that involves taking a dob of butter, putting it on one end of the bread and giving three meticulous swipes to spread it. He's trying to show Price. Of course, the second Price tries to spread his, the centre of the slice tears upwards so there's a big hole in it. Bogle snorts with frustration.

Syd's voice suddenly bellows through the PA, interrupting my thoughts. 'Aaah departing five minutes trippa afternoon safari!' He must have got The Tysonmobile up to the car park.

Granny runs in, the croc rolling in her cleavage.

'Ian? Darl, Syd says can you go on The Tysonmobile with them deaf tourists?'

'Sure, Mrs Pocky.'

'And while I remember, if any of yous boys wants overtime, there's as much as you like. We got the Yarradindi Business Association coming on Saturday for a tour an' sausage sizzle. We need all the help we can get.'

I give Bogle and Price a victory sign. Bogle does a thumbs-up. Price does a clenched-fist salute, but he's still got the knife in his hand and just misses clipping Bogle's glasses with it.

Great.

'You're on, Mrs Pocky. I'll take as much overtime as you can give me.'

Well – I might as well be hanged for a sheep as for a lamb.

I head off to The Tysonmobile. Down the hill, Mr Frye's still yelling. I don't blame him. At this moment, Dylan's hurtling towards his house on a tractor. Knowing Pocky tractors, it probably hasn't got brakes.

I jump on The Tysonmobile as Syd's gargling, 'All aborra tour a famous Yarradindi Tiger aaah, a lucky beggas.'

The last passengers haul themselves up and strap themselves into the harnesses. We're off. I translate as we lurch past armies of tourists heading on foot towards the tiger habitat. Terry gives us a cheery thumbs-up as he untangles an old lady from a collapsed Pockyloo.

Syd's commentary consists of telling the history of the area. This turns out to be how six generations of Pockys have been wrecking the land since white settlement. I translate. When he runs out of things to say I lean over to the microphone and point out the different types of gum tree Mrs McClaren showed the Japanese school kids before the tank incident.

Out of the blue Syd yells, 'Aaaah, hold onna hats!' and drives straight towards an enormous puddle. The Tysonmobile rears up in the air and smashes down. People scream. Syd chortles that it's good to see everyone having such a good time, as we bounce towards the swamp. The Tysonmobile's supposed to be amphibious, but knowing the Pockys, I make plans in case we sink. We crash through reeds, then suddenly – we're afloat. A few people applaud. The rest look around casually. Luckily, they don't realize they're taking their lives in their hands.

I check my watch. Syd reckons the tour should get us back to the Safari Park by six. This means I can return to town on The Tysonmobile with the tourists, see Tash for her evening meal break, whizz across to Pilple to drop off the money I've earned so far, then bike back to the Pockys' to do the overtime. If I'm lucky, I can even do an hour's lino scraping for Dad when I get home.

It's actually handy that Tash is at rehearsals all day, even if she is spending a lot of time with that good-looking Günter guy. At least she won't be expecting to see much of me. I check my phone – no buyers for my stuff yet. I tune back in to Syd describing the range of wrecked cars half sunk in the water. He gets quite emotional about the one his mum and dad set alight then chucked in, flaming, to celebrate their fiftieth wedding anniversary.

Now we're coming towards dry land at the spot where Terry said the Pockys had their family barbies. The engine roars. Syd shouts for everyone to get their cameras out because this is where the tigers are. I translate. We hit firm ground, bounce up the path, then grind to a halt with a scream of brakes. The tourists pile out, cameras at the ready. Syd warns them not to feed the tigers, since it's completely forbidden by the Parks and Wildlife Department.

Except there aren't any tigers. There's not even a bird.

We wait.

And wait.

Finally, a plane flies over. Syd points it out hopefully, but the tourists are unimpressed, so he chuckles nervously and says the tigers must have gone into town to see the tourists, the cheeky beggas. People smile politely.

We wait some more. Syd grins around anxiously. 'Aaaah. Any questions abourra Yarradindi Tiger, a cheeky begga?'

An old man at the back of the crowd says, 'How many hundreds of thousands of years do you estimate the tiger has been here?'

Syd lowers his voice dramatically. 'Millions. Prob'ly squillions. Willions. Prob'ly willions a years, a cheeky begga, taking sausage offa caveman . . .'

People up the back are murmuring, 'Willions?'

But Syd's in full flow. Now he's up to stabillions.

I cut in hastily. 'In fact, scientific research has only just started on the tiger and—'

A man at the front interrupts. 'Look here, it said in the brochure advertising this place that there was a qualified naturalist employed at the Yarradindi Safari

Park, and I don't consider a twelve-year-old boy a suitable substitute . . .'

Twelve?

There's a sudden shriek. While the tourists were listening to Syd, a mangy old tiger's come out of the bush and nipped an elderly lady's ankle. Syd cheers up no end. The tourists are snapping pictures like crazy. Remembering Terry's cheerful tales to Dad about how the tigers were famous for chomping thumbs off to the knuckle, I hurry the tourists back on board.

Syd starts the engine with a mighty roar and we go bouncing off. He says it's good the tiger turned up, because there seem to be fewer and fewer coming out these days, the wily beggas. I say, maybe the noise of the tourists is scaring them off. He shakes his head and gargles that noise never affected them in the past.

Not even gunfire.

There used to be a pack of them in this area, and they'd come out and have a go at anyone in sight, regular as clockwork, at the weekly Pocky barbecue. Even recently, in the early days of the walking tours, one tiger swallowed the end of Mr Frye's boot.

As we crash through protected prehistoric plant life, he confides that it's the lack of tigers that made him buy The Tysonmobile – although he hasn't told the family how worried he is. His idea was that if he could take the tourists deeper into the tiger land, they'd be more likely to see some. The problem is, if the tigers go, the tourists go. And if the tourists go, the town's in deep trouble. What's more, everyone in town will blame the Pockys. This is why it's so important that the Yarradindi Business Association sees tigers on the tour this Saturday.

Syd sighs anxiously. 'Norra Pockys a blame a no tigers! Living two hunner years a tigers.'

He's got a point. The tigers and the Pockys have been living next to each other for centuries without a problem. In fact, having to deal with the Pockys on a daily basis has probably made the tigers a darn sight faster on their feet. It's certainly had that effect on everyone at school. No, whatever's happening, it's only started happening recently. Syd changes gears and shakes his head. 'Aaah, knowa tigers, Ian. Somonna wrong.'

Something *is* wrong at this moment. But not with the tigers. It's a man yelling from the hillside above us, shouting and shaking his fist. It's Mr Frye, of course, leaning over the fence that divides his land from the Pockys' and, surprise, he doesn't like The Tyson-mobile.

I sink down as low as I can in my seat. Syd, mean-while, waves cheerily and blasts the horn. 'Cheeky begga a Mr Frye, allus shouting a joking about!'

It's amazing the way the Pockys never understand that Mr Frye hates them. As his yells recede into the distance Syd says how worried he is about Mr Frye, now Frye's not working at the Safari Park. How can he be coping if the only money coming in is from Mrs

Frye's overseas bat tours, and people visiting their cottage?

We swing into the car park.

Syd leans over, 'Maybe you 'ave a worda him. Maybe gedim aborra Tysonmobile as tour leader, a cleva begga!' He lowers his voice affectionately. 'Tell him, you say, a Pockys warrim back.'

I smile weakly.

As I head back to the kitchen, I hear yelling and shouting. Inside, Price and Bogle are watching in amazement as Dylan and Chett have a fight. But, you've got to know, this isn't just normal Pocky violence. Dylan and Chett really seem to hate each other.

Chett's waving a meat cleaver and yelling as Crusher holds him back. Meanwhile, Dylan's dancing round the kitchen cackling as Terry tries to shut him up. Bogle explains that Dylan trashed some cake Chett had to make for the chef's course he's doing. Apparently, Terry was just telling Chett how good the cake looked when Dylan came in and punched his fist right into it. I make a mental note to stay clear of Chett's cakes. Particularly when he's near that cleaver.

We never get to see how it all turns out because just then Syd appears and takes us through to the cash register in the cafe. He opens it, pays us one hundred and twenty dollars and heads back to adjudicate over the cleaver.

I mutter, 'Sweet.'

Bogle snorts as he gets on his bike. 'Yep. Only a

few million bucks to go. We'll see what games we can sell.'

Price waves. They pedal off just as Terry appears, saying that I can come back tonight to do a couple of hours' overtime re-attaching the basins in the eco-cottages to the bathroom walls. It seems they're inferior foreign basins, so don't attach properly.

This will bring us up to one hundred and forty dollars, plus our ninety dollars, then there's Dad's lino-stripping. I might have a job persuading Mum and Dad to let me start doing the lino at eleven o'clock at night, but it is the holidays. Some holidays.

Still, things are looking up. And just as I'm lurching back to town with Syd on The Tysonmobile, Ruby from The Folders rings me up and says she wants to buy some of my stuff. Excellent. The bad news is that the only time she can make it is at half past seven. So I'll have to leave Tash practically as soon as I arrive. At least I'm seeing her. Syd lets me off The Tysonmobile at the back of Joey's and I dart round to the front. I'm only ten minutes late.

Tash is with a whole bunch of kids. She looks fantastic. I rush up, just in time to hear her say to Günter, 'So this water tank goes rolling down the hill right into our house!'

Uh-oh.

She turns to me. 'Ian, you'll never guess. The Pockys – I can't believe this – they deliberately crushed our garden with a water tank. Then they brought down a tractor and smashed up what was left . . .'

I do profound surprise.

'Oh?'

Günter chips in. 'That's very terrible, poor Natasha. Should you perhaps go home to see all iss OK?'

I feel a surge of jealousy. He's pretty darn fast to get in on the act. I step a bit closer to her. 'Or shall *I* go to your place and make sure it's OK?'

She hugs me. 'No, no. Dad'll be fine. I'm just letting off steam. Let's change the subject. What have you been doing?'

I beam desperately.

'Oh. Nothing. I was . . . just . . . ripping up some lino in the porch for Dad.'

We chat for a couple of minutes. Any moment now I'll have to leave to meet Ruby.

'Ian, why d'you keep looking at your watch?'

'Am I? I . . . sorry. I just . . . I've got to go.'

'But you've only just got here.'

'I promised my dad.'

I get up to hide my guilt. She looks disappointed, but kisses me and says, 'See you at nine o'clock.'

'What?'

'When we finish. We're all going to Dink's.'

I stare at her. 'Dink's?'

'Hello? Earth to Ian? The "get to know you" thing for music camp. I told you this morning.'

9

I've done it again. Because I was happy this morning, I stopped listening. I was just ticking over. What am I going to do? If I go I lose the twenty dollars overtime. But I can't not go – not after rocking up late and having to leave early. I beam. 'Right, OK, see you,' and head off in a flat panic.

I ring Terry to tell him I can't come, rush home, grab a bunch of CDs and run back to the shopping mall.

Ruby's already there with a line of Folders. The whole meeting is conducted with The Folders in full clamp position. You wonder they don't get permanent pins and needles. Ruby buys most of my CDs (and pays me for my skateboard, to give to her brother for his birthday). I hand the CDs over with a pang.

Still, Tash's worth it.

I count the proceeds. Eighty dollars. It's daylight robbery, but it's going to a good cause. I start for Pilple's.

As I'm turning the corner next to the car park Bogle

texts me. He's sold some games. What a mate. I'll pick up the money from his place on the way.

When I get there he reaches into his pocket and pulls out ninety dollars. I'm stunned.

'Bogle . . . what did you sell?'

'Forget it. Just take it to Pilple before I fall to the ground and start chewing the doormat with grief.'

I punch him on the shoulder. I'm cheering up. By the time I've given Pilple this, we'll have paid off three hundred and forty dollars. With a bit of luck, maybe we can earn enough for the whole deposit by the end of tomorrow. Then he can start fixing the cello the morning after.

He answers the door holding half a violin. The weird cabbagey smell wafts out. He scowls as I hand over the money, mutters, 'I hope this girl's worth it. They usually aren't,' and slams the door.

I set off down his driveway, past his dirty old car. Someone's written 'Clean me' on the back window. Now there's a thought. I ring his doorbell again.

'Would you like your car cleaned?'

'How much?'

'Twenty dollars.'

I end up doing it for five. Pathetic. But it's another five dollars closer to the end of all this.

I run to Dink's. As I screech to a halt outside, I can see Tash sitting next to Günter. I'm going to have to watch him. I stroll in as casually as I can. And bump straight into Dink himself.

He scowls down at me, runs his fingers through his greasy hair and growls, 'What are ya having?'

I swear violently to myself. Luckily, I find some coins in my jacket.

I order peppermint tea, which is the cheapest thing on the menu and which I hate. Dink sets it in front of me. It's a cup of warm water with a teabag floating in it. Just as I'm thinking how horrible it looks, he picks out the teabag with his little finger crooked, squeezes it in the cup and puts it in his apron pocket.

Peppermint tea and oil from Dink's sweaty fingers. Tasty.

Tash and the rest of them all start on about their rehearsals. I can't join in, so I sit there, vaguely smiling. I don't understand a word of what they're saying.

Günter chuckles, 'Vat about that pissy car-toe section!'

What section?

They're all chuckling. Tash says, 'He went ballistic!'

Günter laughs. 'Zen all the voodvind came in late.'

Tash is packing up with laughter. 'But the pissy car-toe section – it sounded terrible. I nearly died. Amanda was laughing, so that set me off. Then Günter starts in . . .' Tash sees I'm a bit left out. 'You should have been there, Ian. There's this really hard pissy car-toe bit . . .'

I wish I could join in, say something. I can't just sit here and let musical genius fink-head Günter run the conversation. And Tash seems pretty worried about this car-toe thing.

There's a moment's silence. I smile, squeeze her hand and say encouragingly, 'Oh well. I bet it wasn't that pissy.'

They all stare blankly.

Tash says, 'What wasn't pissy?'

Uh-oh. What have I said?

'The car-toe.' I feel a rush of panic. 'You said it was pissy. I was just saying, well, I bet it wasn't that bad.'

There's a pause. Suddenly, the whole lot of them start rolling about with laughter. Oh no, what have I said? *What have I said?* Tash has got tears running down her face. She grabs my hand.

'Ian. It's not pissy car-toe. It's *pizzicato* . . .' She explodes again. 'It's Italian. It means plucking the string with your finger. But I tell you what, it was definitely seriously pissy.'

They're all howling with laughter, particularly Günter. Great. Made myself look a total moron. I beam brightly.

From then on, my nickname's 'Pissy'. Things go from bad to worse. I don't dare say anything more in case I put my foot in it.

To add insult to injury I'm starving. Some German kid orders steak and chips and leaves half of it uneaten on the plate right under my nose. After about a quarter of an hour, in total desperation I sneak a cold chip. Günter notices. Instead of just sneering, which I could put up with, the rat makes a big fuss out of buying me a plate of chips which I have to eat, thanking him and smiling, because Tash comments that it's such a kind gesture.

I'll give him a gesture if he comes near me. Not a kind one.

Finally, to cap everything, Tash gets a call on her mobile from her mum, who's somewhere in Canada. She goes outside to take it. Without missing a beat, into her chair dumps down a girl with wild black hair and staring eyes. She looks at me from under enormous black eyebrows and says, 'Bree. Percussion. Give me a rhythm.'

'*What?*'

She peers out from under the eyebrows and explains that she can play eight different sorts of drum, plus the xylophone. She can do a different rhythm with each hand, each foot, and her head, all at the same time. She can also sing really high and really low. Just to prove it, she launches into Abba's 'Waterloo' in a big bass voice.

It's like I'm going mad. It gets even more demented because right in the middle of the tune she suddenly starts banging out wild rhythms with her hands and feet and jerking her head about. She looks like she's having some kind of seizure.

Tash comes back after what seems like hours. But because Bree's taken her seat she has to squeeze in among all the German exchange students. Surprise,

surprise, Günter's suddenly sitting next to her. Bree leans over and asks me if I've got any requests.

Like, get out of my face, you wacko.

When I say I haven't, she does the music from *Lord of the Rings: The Two Towers*, accompanying herself by slapping different rhythms on her thighs.

The girl is stark raving mad. How can I get rid of her? I try ignoring her. I try scowling at her. Every time Tash looks my way I smile sweetly. The last thing I want after the pissy incident is for her to think I can't get on with her friends at all. Günter, meanwhile, is now into a range of jokes involving the word 'pissy'.

Well ha-ha-hardy-ha-ha, you big dork.

This is hopeless. I'm counting the minutes until I can get home and do some work for Dad. Finally, at ten past ten, Bree says they have to go. I jump up straight away. They all look at me, so I immediately sit down. As everyone's getting their coats on, Tash whispers, 'Are you OK? You're looking worried. What's the matter?'

Before I can stop myself, I say it.

'Nothing.'

10

'No, tell me, come on.'

I could bite my tongue off. How could I be so stupid?

Never say 'nothing.' It's girl language for 'I have an enormous problem that you've got to interview me to find out about'. I'll have to think of something deep and emotional or she'll keep going till she gets the truth.

She's smiling gently. 'Ian? What is it?'

What can I tell her? I have to say something now she's actually talking to me at last. I stare at her blankly then, in utter desperation, mutter, 'My auntie.'

'Your auntie?'

My auntie?

I cough. 'Yes, she's not well, and I, you know, feel pretty close to her, Auntie Pat . . .'

'What's wrong with her?'

'Oh well. General stuff. Um. Marriage problems mostly.'

How did I get on to Auntie Pat? She's healthy as a crocodile and Uncle Nick's dead. *Dead?* I just said they had marriage problems. Well, I s'pose death's a marriage problem. Pretty serious marriage problem.

I murmur, 'Anyway. It's not important.'

She stares at me in admiration.

'Ian, you are *such* a nice person. That's so kind, worrying about your auntie.'

I smile sheepishly and do my kindest look. Close call.

She cuddles up, kisses me, then adds, 'Hey, I know what'll cheer you up. There's a party at Bree's tomorrow night. Want to come?'

Another night without overtime?

I splutter, 'I can't.'

'Can't. Why not?'

I'm floundering. 'I . . . well . . . Auntie Pat . . .'

Not Auntie Pat again.

'Rudie, Auntie Pat wouldn't want you to be worrying like this.'

'Well, you know, I . . .'

'Trust me. She'd be really upset to know you were this worried. And so would your uncle. It's their problem. They need to sit down together and work it out.'

I get an image of Auntie Pat exhuming Uncle Nick's corpse.

'Now. Please. Come to the party.'

I'll go. I've got to, with Günter sniffing around. I'll get the money somehow.

I beam. 'OK.'

She grins and kisses me.

'OK. I'd better go. See you at lunchtime tomorrow.'

Lunch?

'I . . . well, I . . .'

'What's the matter? Can't you come to lunch?'

I stutter, 'I'll text you . . .' and hurry off. I don't dare stay there any longer or she'll get the truth out of me. At least I can do some lino stripping for Dad. I wish I hadn't made up that stuff about Auntie Pat. Why Auntie Pat? – an asteroid could wipe out the entire solar system and Auntie Pat would be sitting on a chunk of debris in deep space singing the Beatles.

At home, the first thing I see is Terry's ute, stacked with Pockyloos and Ripperson parked in our yard. Ripperson's upper lip curls. According to Terry, this is Ripperson smiling.

Inside, Terry's with Dad. The floor's still covered with torn bits of lino and Terry's unwinding the power cord on an enormous floor-sanding machine. Mum's watching, Daisy in her arms.

Dad turns round and grins. 'G'day, Ian. Terry's helping me strip the floor.'

Blast. If Terry's machine does all the stripping I won't get the money.

Terry looks up proudly from the machine. 'Ya ready, Pete?'

'Yep.'

'Give us the juice.'

Dad puts the plug in. Terry flicks a switch on the machine. Nothing happens. Terry kicks it. Suddenly,

76

the machine roars like a motorbike and takes off on its own across the porch. Spinning wildly, it hits a pile of cardboard boxes, falls over, still spinning, and starts gouging a hole in the skirting board.

Terry rushes across and turns it off.

He tuts and looks up. 'Belt's slipped. I knew it. Darn foreign rubbish. Don't worry, Jan. Be up with me wood filler Sunday.'

Mum gives him a look, sniffs and stalks out.

Terry looks at Dad.

'Women! Can't live with a bitta mess!'

Dad smiles weakly. I can see him thinking that Mum is going to make a serious mess of him after Terry's gone. But Terry's stripper's saved my job.

'Dad, want any help?'

'Too right, mate. Anything to clear up all this.'

He chucks me something that looks like a giant paint stripper. As Terry takes apart the machine, Dad and I get down on all fours and hack and rip at the lino by hand. Terry's told Dad that I'm working up at the Safari Park. I snatch at the first explanation I can think of, which is that I want to buy *Cemetery Trashers IV*.

Terry goes on about the Business Association coming to the Safari Park on Saturday for its special sausage sizzle and tour. It's going to be very posh. The Pockys will need every waiter they can get, so they're glad of me, and Pricey and Bogle. Crusher's making ninety-five meringues for dessert. He's got some mates in the Prison Service to loan him a massive barbecue to cook a range of famous Pocky sausages. These will include the new beer, apple and beef variety, as well, of course, as the traditional beer and Vegemite.

Dad snorts. 'The Business Association is a bunch of snobs. Dunno why you want to be part of it. Specially since you can't join unless you get ten members to vote you in.'

Terry looks up from the pile of screws, nuts and oddly shaped bits of metal and shakes his head.

'Na, you see, Pete, you get to a certain point in your life, you wanna give something back to the community. I mean, the Pockys bin contributing to this town for two hundred years as builders and farmers. Now we're moving into management and tourism, really running the place. We wanna *shape* the town, you know? Put our mark on it.'

Personally, I'd say the town's got the Pockys' marks all over it, particularly in terms of graffiti.

Terry says he'll come back tomorrow with a new belt for the sander.

I take Dad's eight dollars and drag myself to bed. I'm exhausted.

The next thing I know the alarm's going and Syd's warming up The Tysonmobile outside. It sounds like he's about to launch a space shuttle.

At breakfast, Mum's spooning cereal into Daisy's mouth. I wish someone would spoon cereal into my mouth.

Ah, Tash . . .

Maybe I *should* have lunch with her today. But how would I get the overtime money?

We bounce off on The Tysonmobile to pick up the morning tour people from the station. Syd keeps up a cheerful gargle of welcome as I take their tickets.

We surge off down the street, briefly mounting the pavement. Once we get to the freeway, he tells me more about Terry's ambitions to join the Yarradindi Business Association. Syd reckons Terry should have got in last year, and only didn't because he upset some people at a council meeting by yelling, 'Here's the old mare!' and doing clippety-clop noises when Mrs McClaren came in. Which was all in fun and no reason to have him physically thrown out.

We arrive at the Safari Park to see two elderly men wrestling a third out of a collapsed Pockyloo. I go into the kitchen to pick up Syd's thermos of tea. Pricey and Bogle are buttering bread. Chett's cooking bacon, wearing his chef's outfit.

As I enter he looks up at me and hisses, 'In the cold room.'

Once we're inside he looks over his shoulder, turns to me and mutters hoarsely, 'Dylan's hair.'

'What?'

'Get me a bit an' I'll give you fifty dollars.'

'For a bit of his hair? Why?'

'He's got to pay for trashing my cake.'

'But why d'you want his hair?'

'D'ya hear that rain last night?'

I didn't, but I nod.

He jabs himself in the chest. 'Me.'

'You made it rain?'

'Yes. Because . . .' I get a close-up of the scraggy whiskers on his chin as he leans over me menacingly, '. . . I am a witch.'

11

Right. OK.

This is all I need. Chett Pocky is not only dumb and violent, but he thinks he's got supernatural powers. What do you say?

I smile brightly. 'Awesome. Like Harry Potter. You got a broomstick?'

He grabs me by the collar. 'You dissin' me? I'll get a broomstick and stuff it down ya throat, ya dis me . . .'

'No, no. I was just saying.'

He rummages in his pocket, gets out a fifty-dollar note and holds it under my nose.

'One snip. Fifty bucks. Think about it.'

I am thinking about it. I'm thinking it's exactly what I need. I'm also thinking of what Dylan would do to me if he saw me coming at him with a pair of scissors.

Outside, Syd's leaning on the horn of The Tyson-mobile.

I grab his thermos flask, push past Chett, scuttle out to The Tysonmobile and we lurch off. What would Dylan do if he caught me? He'd probably kick off by grabbing the scissors and cutting off every hair on my head.

And I mean 'kick off'.

He'd be kicking me all round the Safari Park, bald and battered. I can't do it. It's impossible.

But, fifty bucks . . . !

We pass Terry at the Pockyloos, extracting a skinhead. Terry's T-shirt reads: 'Don't be a berk, let Pocky and Son do your household maintenance work'.

At the tiger territory, it's worse than yesterday. This time we only glimpse the moth-eaten tiger that turned up yesterday, way off in the distance. Apart from that there's nothing. Syd says he can't understand it. He tells the tourists about the old days when you had to come down here every couple of months and blast around with shotguns just to keep the numbers manageable. Now you're not even allowed to pick off the stragglers. As the tourists' jaws drop, I remember stuff Tash told me about how scientists sometimes have to cull individual animals for the good of the species, and say that it was only the culling done by the Pockys that kept the tigers in such good condition.

A tourist up the back sneers that if the tiger we saw was healthy, he wouldn't like to see a sick one. There's a big roar of laughter. I pretend not to hear.

We go deeper into the bush, but still no luck. Syd's panicking and going into mad chortle mode, but I try to put a brave face on it. Amazingly, all the stuff Tash goes on about to do with animal conservation rushes back to me. I'd no idea I remembered so much.

I say wisely that at certain seasons the tigers migrate to other parts of the bush. The smart alec up the back yells, 'Why are you taking us here, then?'

More roars of laughter.

At least he's giving the tourists a good time. We go even deeper, but eventually the track's so overgrown that people up the back are complaining about getting hit by overhanging branches. Syd apologizes in a wild gargle that mystifies everyone. We turn back.

As we chug across the swamp he turns to me and mutters, 'Warra do a Yarradindi Business Association, a picky beggas?'

But I'm not really listening. Now I don't have to worry about tigers, my mind's gone back to that fifty dollars. Do I dare? Do I have a choice? How many more offers of fifty bucks will come out of the blue? I'll do it, even if it kills me. Which it probably will. Except I'll have to do it before I lose my nerve, like now. I text Tash that I'm not coming to lunch.

Instantly, she rings back. Darn. Now I'll have to think of an excuse.

I put on a bright voice, but she's clearly ticked off. 'Aren't you coming?'

'No, I . . . I'm a bit tied up.'

'Tied up?'

'Yeah, I . . . What with, you know . . . Auntie Pat . . .'
Got to stop about Auntie Pat.

Syd revs The Tysonmobile up a gear.

'What's all that noise?'

'Noise?'

'Yes, I can hardly hear you.'

'Traffic. I'm helping Dad.'

'Wouldn't he let you off for lunch?'

'No, I don't think so.'

'Course he would. You've got to eat.'

'No, I mean, yes he would, but . . . I need the money. I'm saving up. To buy a copy of *Cemetery Trashers IV*.'

'*Cemetery Trashers*? But . . . I thought you hated that game.'

'No, I . . . I've really got into it recently. Funny. It grows on you. Like, at first I really hated it. Now, I . . . You know . . .'

I tail off. There's a silence. I can hear her thinking it's pretty slack that I prefer working to buy some dumb computer game to seeing her. I feel terrible, but what can I do? If I want to go to the party tonight I've got to raise some serious money beforehand.

I change the subject brightly. 'So what's happening with you?'

'Nothing. That stupid school cello's playing up again. I've had to replace a string. I still don't understand Pilple. Why didn't he tell anyone he was going off like that?'

'I know. It's . . . it's . . . weird.'

'Maybe he's back. You know, I think I might go round there in my lunch break tomorrow . . .'

Oh no!

'No way! I mean, no *need*! I dropped in this morning, just in case. The woman next door says he rang and told her he's not coming back for days.'

'That is so slack.'

She raves on about how unreliable Pilple is and how she'll meet me at Dink's before the party, then – relief – she hangs up.

Phew. This isn't good – she's seriously miffed, and who can blame her? On the bright side, at least I stopped her from going round to Pilple's. Now all I've got to worry about is getting stabbed to death by Dylan with my own scissors.

As The Tysonmobile pulls into the car park I jump down and belt into the kitchen. Chett's in the cold room.

I take a deep breath. 'You're on.'

He smiles through his raggedy bristles and gets a pair of scissors out of his tracksuit trousers. 'He's round the back of that shed, painting Pockyloos. And remember . . .' He narrows his eyes. 'I know enough spells to get you as well as Dylan.'

That's a new one. In debt for over a thousand dollars, not seeing my girlfriend for two weeks, having some German musical genius after her, having to pretend I'm worried to death about my super-cheerful Auntie Pat and her dead husband, having to make out I'll die if I don't get some computer game I hate and now having a spell put on me. I resist the urge to ask if he's gonna turn me into a toad.

The way my life's going at the moment it'd be a whole lot easier if I was a toad.

I head off for the shed where The Pockyloos are kept, fingering the scissors in my pocket.

I'm going to cut off Dylan Pocky's hair!

Panic surges in me, but I gulp, think of Tash, and march round the side of the shed. I stop in my tracks – The Pockyloos . . . ! Instead of their normal dark green, they're every colour you can think of. They're even striped. Terry, beaming, and carrying some paint cans, appears with Dylan, who immediately snarls and gives me the finger. My stomach somersaults.

'Whatcha think, Ian?' Terry dumps down the paints and grins triumphantly. 'It's a new concept. Themed for the occasion. It come to me a coupla nights ago. See, other Portaloos, they're all the same. But ours! If it's a wedding, white. If it's a party, red and yellow stars.' He puts a pot of paint and a brush in my hand. 'Special order from the mobile blood bank. Five red ones. You paint 'em, Dyl screws 'em together.' He grins. 'And no skylarking about. I know you two!'

Terry and Syd have this fantasy that I'm best mates with the Pocky kids. The truth is they've been attempting grievous bodily harm on me since the first day I set foot in town. To prove the point, behind Terry's back Dylan curls his lip savagely and jabs the air with his screwdriver.

This is a bad, bad idea.

As Terry leaves to sort out a tourist who's been hit by a falling noticeboard, Dylan sticks his face in mine and growls, 'One wrong move – I'll get ya.'

I smile brightly.

We set to work. Dylan has to drill holes in the doors then put on hinges. I sneak a professional look at his head. It's strangely pointy. In a few thousand years' time a bunch of archaeologists will dig up that skull and think he belongs to a different species.

He probably does.

But the good thing is that a lock of shining blond hair is dangling down the back of his neck. That's my baby. When he's not looking, I whip the scissors out of my pocket, hide them behind my back and creep across to him. My heart's thumping. I'm so close I can see the sweat on his neck. I lean across, lift the scissors . . .

He swings round!

I clamp the scissors behind my back just before he sees them. I'm so close our noses are nearly touching. The blood's beating inside my ears. I beam innocently. He glares at me.

'What you doing?'

'Doing?'

'What you up so close for?'

'I was just . . . seeing how you drill.'

He jabs his ferrety face into mine.

'The way ya drill, dog-breath, is ya stick the drill in the wood and pull the trigger.'

'Oh. Yeah. Right.'

I go back to painting. He gives me a suspicious look, licks his lip ring and turns back to his doors. How did I get into this? Time is ticking away. As I'm painting, I inch up casually. Closer. I lift the scissors . . .

Now!

I lunge for the hair. But in my panic I kick a paint can and he hears and spins round. I try to put the scissors behind my back, but he's seen them. He grabs me and sticks the screwdriver up my left nostril.

'Ya runt, you're tryna kill me!'

I wriggle free and charge off. I'm dodging and bobbing in and out of The Pockyloos.

'Come 'ere, I'll kill you.'

He's chasing me, grabbing at me and swearing. I dart behind a stacked heap of wooden doors and crouch down. Silence. More silence. He's gone.

Eh? Where is he?

Doubled over, I sneak round the side of the nearest Pockyloo – right into him.

12

Oh no!

Dylan wrestles me for the scissors. He gets them. He's going to stab me. This is it, Dylan's going to kill me. Frantic, I snatch up a paint brush and dob him right on the nose. He stops in surprise.

'What? You . . .'

Eyes burning, he chucks down the scissors, snatches a paint brush and dobs me on the nose.

I dob his cheek.

He dobs my cheek.

This is bizarre. We're taking it in turns to dob each other. It's like some kind of ping-pong match. But any minute he's going to stop dobbing and start thumping. I've got to do something. Desperate, I seize my chance and swing a wild punch and . . . amazingly, he goes 'Oomph', and keels over, clutching his stomach. What?

I decked Dylan Pocky?

Decking Dylan Pocky's everyone's dream – and everyone's nightmare. Pocky revenge tactics are legendary.

This is no time to stand around. I career off like a maniac. Straight into Syd.

'Aaah! Cheeky beggas, play up a minute a back's turned aaah!'

I've never been so pleased to see anyone in my life. He wants me to come on the next Tysonmobile tour, as soon as I've washed my face. I'm right on his heels. As I look back, Dylan's still on the ground hugging his stomach. I can't believe I decked Dylan Pocky. And I still didn't get the hair.

Bogle appears from the cold room carrying a computer monitor. Eh? But this is the Pockys' – anything's possible. 'Why you covered in paint?'

I stick my head under a tap outside the toilet block.

'Long story. Basically, Chett's a witch and I just punched out Dylan Pocky.'

'*What?*'

At that moment Chett comes out of the kitchen and grabs me by the collar.

'D'ya get it?'

'Not yet.'

'Get me that 'air – or I'll rip your nose off!'

'Chett. Um. Just one thing.'

'What?'

'I lost the scissors.'

He lets out a stream of swear words and heads off to the kitchen.

Bogle's standing there with his mouth open.

'What's with the scissors?'

'Voodoo. He's paying me fifty bucks to get a lump of Dylan Pocky's hair.'

'Have you gone totally insane? Dylan's hair? He'll kill you. And what d'you mean, you punched him out?'

The reality of what I've done hits me like a bucket of cold water. Not only have I made an enemy of Dylan Pocky, the person in town most likely to end up on *Australia's Most Wanted Criminals*, but I've still got to chop off a chunk of his hair. What's more, the person I've got to give it to is the person in town who's second most likely to end up on *Australia's Most Wanted Criminals*.

How can I do it? Could I do it when he's asleep? Could I drug him? How *do* you drug someone anyway? People are always doing it on TV, but what's the practical side of it? I can hardly walk into the chemist's and ask for something to knock Dylan unconscious for half an hour. Mind you, if it was possible, half the school would jump at the chance, particularly the teachers.

'Rude.' It's Bogle, and he's genuinely worried. 'You can't do this. It's suicidal.'

'Stop freaking me out.'

'You need to be freaked out. What if he comes round that corner and gets you?'

My stomach's doing cartwheels of panic.

Chett reappears. 'Use these.'

He's clutching a gigantic pair of scissors with serrated edges.

I blink. 'What the heck are those?'

'They're for cutting up chooks.'

'Chickens? They look like you could use 'em to knacker an elephant. Don't you think he'll see me coming?'

He grabs me by the collar again.

'You dissing me?'

'No, no, I . . .'

'It's all I could find, now take 'em!'

He gives me a shake, shoves me and slouches off. Bogle looks at me.

'Rude, you are the most disaster-prone person I've ever met.'

'I'll be even more disaster-prone if I don't get that bit of hair.'

I'm about to stick the scissors down the front of my jeans when Bogle points out that I could do myself a mischief. I put them down the back. It makes me walk like a duck, but at least if there's an accident I'll only slice off a buttock.

By now Syd's blasting the hooter of The Tysonmobile.

I do up my belt. 'That's Syd. I've got to go on the afternoon tour. I'll get the hair later.'

Bogle throws up his hands. 'No way! You got to get out of it!'

'It's fifty bucks!'

He's spluttering with frustration. 'Even if you get away with it, how are you going to stop him coming to get you afterwards? I mean . . . *Dylan Pocky*, man! D'you think you should leave town?'

I lean into his face. 'Know what I like about you, mate? You never panic.'

Of course, he's now got me into a total sweat. Even if I get the hair, how can I lay low when I'm working in the same place as Dylan? I get an image of myself stretched out dead next to the toilet block.

With the scissors down my pants it's hard to hurry. I waddle as fast as I can past Auntie Meryl tying Syd and Granny's dog Ripper to a post next to Ripperson. It's a shame there isn't a dog around with the right sort of hair. I could snip a bit and Chett would never know. The scissors slip down my leg. I nip behind a shed to readjust them without people seeing me. That's all I need, people at school finding out I had scissors down my pants. What do I say as an excuse? That this is what I normally do in moments of boredom?

Terrific. I'd be the school pervert.

Meanwhile, tourists are pouring on to The Tysonmobile. I hear Terry saying, 'Course, at this point a time I don't think I'm experienced enough to be a committee member of the Business Association, like a seccatary for instance . . .' and a familiar voice rings out, 'The correct pronunciation is "*secre*tary", Mr Pocky. I'm not sure of the origin of the term, but possibly it had something to do with keeping secrets.'

Not Mrs McClaren . . . What's she doing back? She's with a bunch of French students and, surprisingly, the new mayor, who runs the Mercedes Benz dealership in town. He's giving Terry snooty looks as Terry explains all the features of The Tysonmobile.

Syd's looking on anxiously. He obviously had no idea he'd have to take out the mayor today. He's sweating on it.

Finally, everyone's on. Mrs McClaren and the French kids have taken seats in the middle. The new mayor sniffs bossily and deliberately takes my seat next to Syd to show how important he is. I'm forced to go up the back behind Mrs McClaren. As Terry waves goodbye, Syd looks over his shoulder and gives me an anxious look. Meanwhile, Mrs McClaren is being her usual irritating self. She's getting the poor French kids to think of good ways to describe being hungry in English.

One of them says, 'As hungry as a cow with two stomachs.'

Mrs McClaren explains that actually cows have four stomachs, and gives all their scientific names. She is so annoying.

I glare at the back of her head. Her hair's so sculptured it looks like a helmet. Actually, it looks like my mum's when she's just been to the hairdresser's, although my mum's hair is dark, while Mrs McClaren's is exactly the same blond as Dylan's – except of course Dylan's blond doesn't come out of a bottle.

Wait a minute.

I couldn't.

Why not? Chett would never know. It's not as if he can really do voodoo.

I get a mental picture of Mrs McClaren twitching and jerking about the supermarket as if someone's sticking invisible needles in her.

I get a mental picture of the fifty-dollar note.

Let's do it.

Just as The Tysonmobile is bumping down to the swamp, I whip out the scissors, stand up in my seat and grab a big lump of Mrs McClaren's hair. The snip makes an incredibly loud slicing noise, but Mrs McClaren's so busy asking the French kids to name five different sorts of marsupial she doesn't even notice. One of the kids sees me though. He starts grinning and whispering to the others. I stuff the scissors down the back of my jeans, slip the hair in my pocket and check out Mrs McClaren's gleaming hair helmet. You can see exactly where I snipped. It looks like something took a bite out of her hair. The French kid gives me the victory sign.

I just hope Chett buys it.

We drive into tiger territory. This time there are no tigers at all. The French kids couldn't care less. They're too busy giggling about Mrs McClaren. And Mrs McClaren doesn't seem to care either. She's going on about eucalyptus oil and discussing the state of elephant populations across the planet.

But the new mayor is seriously ticked off. He goes into a big rave about how he's heard that tiger numbers are dropping every day. It's clear he thinks the Pockys are to blame.

Mrs McClaren comes to the rescue, describing the Pockys' noble history as bush-fire fighters. This goes back several generations and involves various Pockys volunteering to go into dangerous situations to put out fires.

Luckily, she doesn't know that the reason the Pockys know so much about fires is because they spend their teenage years setting light to people's letter boxes.

But the mayor won't have the subject changed. He says that the tiger is now the town's major asset, and it's worrying that *certain people* don't have proper respect for that fact, since it's hardly very business-minded. Syd's face falls. He looks at me in desperation.

I feel like saying the only reason that the tigers are there at all is because the Pockys have been neglecting the land and persecuting any wildlife that came in their way for the last two hundred years. Which made the tigers so tough they could stand anything, but I can't really take on the mayor.

I feel bad for Syd.

But I'm stoked that I've got the hair. I check it out. It really looks like Dylan's hair. It's excellent. The big problem now is going to be avoiding Dylan until he's cooled down. If he ever does.

We bounce and roll our way back home. As The Tysonmobile pulls into the car park I sight Dylan in the distance digging a trench.

Uh-oh.

I dart into the kitchen where Chett's rolling pastry and give him the scissors and Mrs McClaren's hair. There's a tense moment while he stares closely at it.

'It's kinda dry-looking.'

I blink innocently. He frowns, turns it over a few times, sighs, then hands me the fifty dollars. Sweet. Now I just have to find a way to stay close to adult Pockys for the rest of the day so that Dylan can't get me.

I dash across to the souvenir shop, where Granny or Crusher should be on duty. They're not, but Price is behind the counter arranging a pile of stuffed tigers.

As soon as Pricey sees me, he starts gabbling.

'Deep trouble, mate. Dylan's asking round for you everywhere. He's gonna kill you for whacking him. And if he doesn't kill you, Chett will, when you don't get him the hair.'

'I got him the hair.'

'*You cut Dylan's hair!*'

'No. Mrs McClaren's. It's the same colour.'

At that exact moment, we're interrupted by a commotion over at the barbecue area. The mayor is shouting at Terry and Mrs McClaren, who are surrounded by a bunch of assorted adult Pockys. Terry's looking bewildered. Mrs McClaren's trying to calm things down. Apparently, it's about Crusher, who's in front of the barbecue ready to serve up a range of Pocky sausages as lunch for the French kids. He's stripped to the waist and running with sweat. From what we can make out, the mayor feels that when Crusher leans across to turn the meat he's probably shedding sweat and bunches of armpit hair all over the food.

He's got a point.

While Pocky men always have a serious amount of curly, reddish-gold fuzz over their entire freckly bodies, particularly in their armpits, Crusher's armpits look like ginger candy floss. Even when his arms are by his sides you can see big shaggy tufts poking out. It looks like he's got a ginger-headed gnome crushed under each armpit and all that's visible is the beards.

The mayor insists that a new batch of sausages is brought out from the kitchen. Granny comes storming into the shop.

'I never heard a such a thing. Tell me where it says anything in the health regulations about a man's pits?'

She works off her rage by organizing the photo exhibition of tattooed elderly bikies on the shop wall, which will eventually go into the Tattoo Hall of Fame that Syd's planning as a special attraction for bikie gangs passing on the nearby freeway.

She looks up from a photo of a man with the Pope's head tattooed on his back and says grimly, 'If a man can't show his pits on a hot day. If a decent man's gonna be persecuted for his normal bodily features . . . ! The Pockys got beaudiful hair, always 'ave done.'

Over at the barbecue, Auntie Barbara Pocky has taken over from Crusher, and Syd's arrived with a new batch of sausages from the cold room. Terry is smiling hopefully at the mayor, who's clearly unimpressed.

Price suddenly hisses, 'Get down, quick!'

It's Dylan. He's walking towards the shop.

13

I duck behind the counter and hear his voice.

'Where's Rude?'

'Dunno, mate, haven't seen him.'

My heart's pounding. After what seems hours, Price finally says, 'OK, he's gone.'

I sigh and get up from behind the counter. I'm a nervous wreck. I'm suddenly aware of Price saying something.

'So, whadya think?'

'About what?'

'What I've been talking about.' He stares at me hopelessly, sweat beading on his red nose. 'I'm gonna do it, mate. I'm gonna go up to her and say . . .' his voice comes out all cracked and squeaky, 'Hi, Ruby.'

He stares at me for approval.

I stare back. What am I going to say?

'Cool, mate . . . Good start.'

Some day I'm going to have to take Price seriously in hand.

Just then, Syd appears on the steps of the cafe, yelling to us. Hallelujah, end of the day.

I check for Dylan and dart across. Bogle's already been paid. Syd hands Price and me our money. I gather it all up and add it to Chett's fifty and the fifty Price got for selling his games.

Yes!

Price and Bogle head for their bikes, waving good-bye. We've now got pretty much enough for Pilple to start work. I'll drop off the money at his place, get changed for the party and spend the evening with Tash. We're on our way, tonight I can relax. At which point I freeze.

It's Mr Frye – crouching behind a stack of broken chairs at the back of the cafe.

He'll go bananas if he knows I'm working for the Pockys. He mustn't see me.

Darn it, he has. But instead of going feral, he puts a finger to his lips and motions me towards him frantically. I suddenly realize. He's hiding. Hiding? What's he up to?

'Mr Frye. About me being here . . .'

'Shh! Quickly, get down.'

I crouch beside him.

He turns his mad eyes towards me. 'You're exactly the person I want to see. These Pockys, they're a menace. I thought I'd seen everything, but now, the last straw, blasting through sensitive wetland areas and pristine bush in an army vehicle. I have to stop this, Ian. I've tried official channels, but no one will listen. So. I've taken matters into my own hands. I've got to save the animals and the rainforest, and I will. Don't worry, I have *plans in motion*.'

He does? What plans? And why's he telling me?

He smiles, his eyes glittering. Any minute now he's going to ask me why I'm here. Why *could* I be here?

I stare round frantically for ideas. *Yes!*

'Mr Frye, I was just on my way to ask you. While Natasha's not here to help you, would you like a hand with the animals?'

His eyes brighten. 'Ian, that's very kind and thoughtful of you. I could really do with some help.'

I smile weakly. It's the good news and the bad news. The good news is that he hasn't realized I'm working for the Pockys. The bad news is that I'll have to spend about an hour helping him, and time is ticking away. I've still got to pay Pilple tonight or he won't start on the cello. And I can't be late for Tash again. Not with Günter lurking about.

For the next hour I clean out reeking animal pens and scrub stinky feeding bowls. Frye raves on about the Pockys. The worst thing is that every time he thinks of something else to complain about, he stops doing what he's doing and just stands there, ranting.

Finally, we're done.

'OK, Mr Frye, I'm off . . .'

'Not yet you're not.' He smiles and reaches into his pocket. 'Here, I insist. Twenty dollars. I met your father this morning and he told me you were saving to buy a computer game.'

102

He smiles affectionately. I feel like a rat.

To make me feel even worse, he gives me a lift home and tells Mum what a great son she has.

I have a shower in record time, shoot out the door and run like a madman to Pilple's. He counts the money agonizingly slowly.

'So, um, Mr Pilple, will you start the cello now?'

'Tomorrow.'

'And . . . I can pick it up on Saturday night?'

'Providing you've paid me the full amount by then.' He narrows his eyes. 'All this for a girl?'

What's his problem with women?

'Er. Yeah.'

He just stares at me. I'm out of here. It's excellent that he's starting, but I'm dreading being late again for Tash. Especially after that phone call. I run all the way to Dink's, lean against the wall outside gasping, then casually stroll in.

'Sorry I'm late, I got held up.'

But Tash is beaming, 'I know you did. I just got a call from my dad saying how you'd gone up there especially to help him with the animals. Rudie, you are so sweet. And –' she kisses me – 'I hope things are going better for Auntie Pat.'

We set off for the party. I'm on one side of Tash, Bree's on the other. Bree's singing boy-band hits and keeping time by banging her hands on her backside. Günter's following behind.

Suffer!

Tash keeps snuggling up and going on about a surprise that she's got for me. Actually, it's strange because, even when she asks me if I want to help set up the chairs for a concert practice run she's got tomorrow afternoon, and I say I've got to work for Dad, she's not annoyed. In fact, she and Bree exchange grins.

Still, who's complaining? I'm really going to enjoy this party. Specially now we've got the cello started. At Bree's, Tash gets me to sit on a couch. She tells me to close my eyes and hold out my hands. She puts something into them.

'Open your eyes.'

I beam and look down.

It's a copy of *Cemetery Trashers IV*.

She's grinning triumphantly. 'It's Bree's. She was given two copies for her birthday. So.' She sits down next to me. 'Now you don't have to work for your dad.'

14

'I can't take it.'

'It's fine, she's got another copy.'

'I want to buy my own.'

'That's ridiculous – she says you can keep it.'

'I want a brand-new copy.'

'What's wrong with you? Why are being so weird? First, you start obsessing about a game you've always hated. Now this.' Her mouth sets in a hard line. She folds her arms. 'It's Bree, isn't it? You've got some-thing against Bree.'

'It's nothing to do with Bree.'

'Bree might be a bit unusual, Ian. She might be a bit full on about rhythms and her eyebrows might be bushy . . .'

'This is nothing to do with Bree . . .'

'. . . but she's got a lot more personality than your "friend" Ruby Pearson and her crowd put together . . .'

'Ruby Pearson?'

'If you took Bree's *Cemetery Trashers* you could come and sit in on the rehearsal tomorrow and I could see you.'

I stare at her helplessly.

'So.' She's grim. 'You'd rather be ripping up lino than spending time with me?'

'Well, you'd rather be at music camp than spending time with me.'

Why did I say that? Where did that come from?

'That's how you feel?'

'No. I don't. I don't. I . . . I just don't want to let down my dad.'

I've got to go. If I don't, she's going to start with more questions.

'Ian?' There's a strange, urgent note in her voice.

'What?'

She stares at me, then looks away. 'Nothing.'

Oh no!

We're into 'nothing' territory. 'Nothing' means 'a whole heap', and I'm supposed to ask her more so we can talk it out. But the longer we keep talking the harder it'll be to stay off the subject of the cello. I've got to get out of here.

I jump up from the couch and gabble, 'See you then. I've got to go and help Dad.'

'*Now? Again?* We've only just got here.'

'Yeah, I . . . I didn't realize what the time was.'

'And I won't see you tomorrow at all?'

She's half-angry, half-sad.

I add desperately, 'But we'll see each other the day after that. We'll do something in the evening together. I promise.' This is seriously risky because it means no overtime, but I've got to keep her off the scent. She just stares at me.

I don't know what to do, so I peck a kiss on her cheek and hurry out. At the door I turn – to see Günter standing next to her talking. Great. I'm practically driving her into his arms. *It's only till Saturday.*

My mobile rings. It's Bogle. 'Where you been? You OK? We thought Dylan'd got you.'

'No. I was helping Natasha's dad with his animals.'

'You were *what*?'

'Long story.'

Bogle sighs. 'As long as you're not in a ditch with your head bashed in. Listen, tomorrow, at the Safari Park. When Dylan's around we'll text you.'

'Thanks, mate. Good idea.' I hang up. An early warning system makes sense.

I turn the corner – and Dylan's coming straight towards me.

'Eh, Ian!'

I run. He runs after me. He's gaining. He corners me next to the post office. My stomach somersaults with panic. I'm trapped. He's going to hammer me.

But he doesn't. There's a strange, twisted shape to his mouth. I realize . . . it's a crooked smile.

He tilts his head, licks his lip ring and says, 'That punch, man. Intense.'

And walks off.

I just stand there. Did I dream that? Was Dylan Pocky being friendly?

That's a worry. Having Dylan as your enemy is bad enough. Having Dylan as your friend could be even worse. Maybe it's some kind of trick. He's lulling me into a false sense of security so he can hammer me twice as effectively as before. I jog home, constantly checking over my shoulder.

At our place Terry and Dad are unloading an even bigger sanding machine in the porch. Terry gave up on the new belt for the old one. He explains that this is the industrial model 2NW, famous for extra horse-power. All we need is hot water poured on the remaining bits of lino and the 2NW will rip it off like the skin off a grape. Mum comes in carrying Daisy and asks how many months this is all going to take.

Terry grins. 'Don't you worry. The minute this little beauty takes over you won't know what's happened to you. Watch this. Give us the water, Pete.'

Dad pours a puddle of hot water on the ripped lino. Terry grins, hits the switch – and the sander shoots off sideways, dragging him with it in wild circles. Dirty water and bits of lino spray everywhere. Daisy's laugh-ing her head off. By the time he wrestles it to a halt, it's gouged a wiggly groove about two centimetres deep into the floorboards. We all stand looking at it.

Terry says, 'See that? Could eat your dinner off them boards.'

Mum says she'll make a point of eating her dinner off the boards from now on. She leaves, jumping to flick a bit of lino off the wall light as she passes. Terry reckons we can fill the gouged bit in with wood filler.

Dad slips me ten dollars to clean up the mess.

Before I go to sleep I try to ring Tash, but her mobile's off. Suddenly, Dylan comes in. He's completely bald and he's yelling that I took his hair. He comes for me with a pair of scissors. Bogle rushes in, saying Pocky hair is worth a fortune on the international hair market.

'Ian? Ian, wake up, you're having a nightmare.'

It's Mum, sticking her head around my door.

'Are you all right? You were shouting – the strangest things! About the Pockys' hair.' She frowns. 'Mind you, the Pockys do have an amazing amount of hair. And so shiny. They must have a lot of yeast in their diet.'

And she's gone. I stare at the ceiling. I'm exhausted before I even get up. There's so many things to worry about – whether Tash will go round to Pilple's, Mr Frye, Dylan. But most of all, Tash herself, who thinks I don't care about her when everything I'm doing is for her and I'm missing her like crazy. I just hope nothing goes wrong and I can see her tomorrow night. I text her all my love.

Only till Saturday.

At breakfast Dad, who does the Pockys' business accounts, mentions that visitor numbers at the Safari Park have been falling over the last week. Mum says she had a bunch of tourists in complaining that the

Pockys' place was a rip-off because they paid for a tiger tour and all they saw was one moth-eaten tiger with a limp.

As I crunch my cornflakes I get flashbacks from my dream. Dylan bald was an amazing sight. Now there's him to avoid as well.

I check my phone. No reply from Tash.

On our way to the station, Syd's going on and on about the lack of tigers. To add insult to injury, the new mayor apparently told Mrs McClaren that at no time are any of the Pockys allowed to show their pits, on the basis that tourists could catch a disease. Which Syd reckons is plain rude, since the Pockys' pits are no worse than any other pits, including the mayor's, and it goes against nature to cover 'em. We load on the tourists and lurch off.

Bogle texts me that Dylan's by the shop, so as soon as I get to the Safari Park I nip into the kitchen. Someone taps me on the shoulder. I nearly jump through the ceiling. But it's Chett in his chef's whites, grinning.

'Get a load a this.' He holds up a little home-made doll. You can tell it's Dylan by the pointy nose and, glued on top of its head, a tuft of blond hair.

Except of course it's not Dylan's hair, it's Mrs McClaren's, and sticking right out of the middle of it is an enormous needle.

I have a vision of Mrs McClaren staggering about, clutching her head while explaining the difference between 'their' and 'there'.

Chett smirks. 'All I gotta do is paint on his socks.'

Just then we hear footsteps and Dylan's voice yelling, 'Rude? Rudie, where are ya?'

Chett hisses, 'Quick, get behind them shelves and watch!'

I'm behind them like a flash.

As Dylan walks in, Chett jumps out, waves the doll, shouts a bunch of weird words and triumphantly stabs the doll all over its body with the needle.

Dylan lands him a mighty punch on the jaw, then turns and sees me. He does his weird smile and says, 'Afta work. Wanna come down the bus station and do graffiti?'

15

Is it . . . can it be . . . ? Dylan wants to . . . *bond*?

Luckily, Crusher calls him off to stack some milk crates, so I don't have to continue the conversation. Syd blasts on The Tysonmobile horn. I step over Chett, head outside and jump on.

OK. Dylan seriously wants to be my friend. Dylan Pocky, chief neighbourhood vandal, wants me to become his sidekick. This means a choice of ending up in kids' jail or hospital, possibly hospital and a kids' jail. And what would Tash think? How am I going to put him off? I suddenly register what Syd's saying. He's saying that Mrs McClaren was round at Terry's last night but had to go home because of a headache.

A headache? Mrs McClaren had to go home because of a headache?

I try to get Syd to tell me more, but now he's on to tigers again. If enough tigers don't turn up, Terry's chances of becoming a member of the Yarradindi Business Association will be wrecked. And if the government starts to think that the Pockys are causing the tigers to go missing, maybe the Safari Park will even be closed. Granny reckons tourist numbers at the Safari Park were seriously down yesterday. It might just be a coincidence, but what if the tourists keep staying away?

I can't stop thinking about the giant needle in the doll's head. What if Mrs McClaren dies?

I suddenly see Mr Frye perched on a hill with binoculars. I duck down and pretend to do up my shoe.

Not him as well. I'm turning into a nervous wreck.

We chug through the swamp, bounce into tiger territory and see – exactly nothing. The tourists get off and stare around. Zero tigers and hardly a bird. Syd tries to make a joke about it. He's so anxious even I find it hard to make out what he's gargling about. I do my stuff about how rare they are, but the tourists aren't happy.

On the way back he keeps going over it. 'Aaaah, donunderstanna wharra wrong a tigers, a mangy beggas. Thinga missing a sausages and scraps a barbecue. Thinga plain hungry. Gone a place a good food, a cleva beggas.'

Dylan's waiting for me in the car park. I explain I don't have enough artistic talent to do graffiti. He says that's OK. We can go down the beach and trip up tourists.

In the background, Chett's frantically stabbing his doll with a kebab skewer.

'Hel-lo, Ian. I see you're having fun with young Dylan.'

It's Mrs McClaren, coming out of the Pocky farm-house.

At least she's still alive.

I'm checking her head for pinholes when she pulls me aside and whispers, 'I'm so pleased you and Dylan are making friends. You can be a *Good Influence* on him. And Mr Frye's been telling me how wonderful you are. You see, Ian . . .' as she turns to check that no one's listening, the big hole in her helmet flops open '. . . when we talk about Dylan, we are talking about . . . an extremely lonely boy.'

Dylan – lonely?

And then it hits me. She's right. Dylan *is* lonely. His best mate and fellow-psychopath from school, Justin, is now working at the abattoirs. His girlfriend Kylie's gone off with a Year 11. His other friends spend their days travelling the trains looking for vandalism opportunities in towns where the police don't know them, which he can't do because he's stuck working for Terry. And the younger Pocky kids, including Clint and Troy, are either off playing havoc on their own or going round with Chett because he's got a car.

Dylan is, actually . . . lonely.

I don't believe it. Still, I s'pose even murderous psychos get lonely – between court appearances. Poor old Dylan!

What am I saying? Dylan's a homicidal maniac.

But Mrs McClaren's still going on. 'The point is, Ian, that you are a born counsellor. People choose you to share their problems. And at this moment you have it in your power to make peace between the Pockys and the Fryes, two families who mean a great deal to you. So, next time you help Mr Frye with his animals . . .' she beams, '. . . I want you to take Dylan.'

Is she insane? Dylan let loose on Mr Frye's animals? I get an image of a hail of fur and feathers.

Terry suddenly appears behind her, looking bewildered. His T-shirt reads: 'Don't you relent, let Pocky and Son deliver your discount cement'.

'Ian, mate, Mrs Mac wants you to help me fix the bog.'

'*Blog*, Mr Pocky.'

She turns to me.

'Ian, I want you to help Mr Pocky create a blog, to show members of the Yarrandindi Business Association all the good work the Pockys are doing out here.'

Terry says, 'It's the spelling I'm worried about—'

I cut him off. 'You want Andy for that, Mr Pocky.'

'Too busy, mate. He's over the museum putting in sound effects so when you walk past the sign on the wall that tells you about Great-Grandpa Pocky getting his hand bit off you get the screams and growling. Lifelike. You're waiting for the tiger to come round the corner with a thumb sticking out his mouth . . . !'

Mrs McClaren bundles me off with Terry into the office. As she leaves, she puts her hand on my arm and whispers, 'And remember, Ian. It's up to people like us to Make a Difference.'

I show Terry how to use spellcheck. I show him how when you type 'Dear' the computer knows you're writing a letter and will help you. I show him autotext, and explain how it's predictive. This way, he can just type in the address of the Safari Park once and give it a few identifying letters, and next time he types those letters and hits 'enter' the whole address will come out automatically.

He's stoked. He says he knew his last two years at school were a waste of time. He tells me that when he's in the Yarradindi Business Association, he'll suggest that they employ me and Bogle as computer experts.

I'm just showing him how to do emails when Syd scuttles in and says he needs me. He's strangely edgy. He hurries me outside through a mob of tourists who've gathered to watch five elderly Pockys try to tow away an ancient rusting truck with Troy sitting on the top. Mrs McClaren's supervising. Every time they try to attach tow chains to the truck, bits of it fall off.

'Where are we going?'

He frowns anxiously and puts his finger to his lips. He takes me to the back of the cafe and hands me a heavy green plastic garbage bag, taking another one himself.

'What's happening?'

He looks at me desperately. 'Have to do it, a silly beggas.'

'Have to do what?'

'Gerra tigers a Business Association.'

'But what have these bags got to do with the Yarradindi Business Association?'

He looks over his shoulder, turns to me wide-eyed with panic and whispers hoarsely, 'Sausages.'

16

'Sausages?'

Is he losing it?

'Inna bag.'

I look inside my green plastic bag. Sure enough, it's packed with cooked sausages.

'But what are we . . .'

'Shhh!'

He puts his finger to his lips, disappears into a shed, reappears with the outboard motor from a boat, then hurries me off towards the swamp, explaining as we go. He's convinced he's worked out the reason the tigers have gone.

For two hundred years the tigers have been relying on the Pocky family for food scraps, so now that the Parks and Wildlife Department have said nobody's allowed to feed the tigers, they're hiding and doing their own thing. The only way to get them back – particularly for when the Yarradindi Business Association comes for its tour – is to give them food. Since their favourite food is Uncle Cec Pocky's original beer and Vegemite sausages, Syd's idea is to hide sausages in strategic places in the wilderness, just until the big tour. He rolls his eyes and murmurs that it's like fate wanted this to happen because today there are mountains of sausages left over from when the mayor banned Crusher from the barbie.

I don't like the sound of this at all.

'What if the Parks and Wildlife people find out?'

What if Tash finds out!

'Howa find out, a silly beggas?' He shrugs in despair. 'Don' lika do 'is, Ian, burr, tellatruth, a desperate.'

He assures me the sausages are only a temporary thing. Once the tigers are back he'll think of a legal way of keeping them there. The main thing now is to get them back as fast as possible, in time for the Business Association tour. If we lay the sausages out quickly, the tigers might even be back before the afternoon safari.

He swears me to secrecy. No way can Terry find out or he'll be furious. Now that he's trying to be part of the Yarradindi Business Association, he wants everything done proper and according to the rules.

'Promise nortella Terry?'

'I promise.'

Not another secret.

We cross the swamp by boat and rush along the track, hiding sausages. I'm so hungry I could eat the sausages myself.

I remember Crusher's pits and think better of it.

When we're done, we jump into the boat and roar back. There's ten minutes to get The Tysonmobile back to town to pick up the tourists for the afternoon safari. Syd guns down the freeway. We hurtle into the station forecourt, pack the grumbling tourists on board and head off. Syd's on tenterhooks. Finally we're bouncing down the hill towards the swamp.

As we get to the other side there's no sign of any tigers. Syd swallows hard, mutters, 'Come out a bush, a silly beggas . . .' drops The Tysonmobile into a lower gear and we chug slowly along. Still nothing happens.

Then, amazingly, there they are! Two of them, through the trees. They're looking a bit decrepid, but still. The tourists 'oo' and 'ah' and whip out their cameras. We chug along some more and – yes! – there's another one, wolfing down something that's got to be a sausage. It bares its teeth and snarls. The tourists are chuckling and chatting. Three tigers. Syd's over the moon. He blasts on The Tysonmobile hooter for good luck, sending roosting bats fluttering.

As we career for home, I check my phone. Still no reply from Tash to my text. I text, 'I love', and stop. Start again, stop and curse frantically under my breath. I'm in a totally no-win situation. I want her to reply, but if she does I'm frightened I'll get my lies tangled up. Which makes me realize: our date tomorrow night. There's no way I can bluff her for a whole evening. I'll have to say I can't make it – though how I can do that without offending her even more than she is already

I don't know. I sigh and snap my phone shut as we bounce, revving, into the car park. Dylan's waiting for me. He suggests we go up the shopping mall and gouge holes in all the phone booths with Stanley knives. I explain I'm busy tonight. He says it's OK, we can do it tomorrow. I say tomorrow I'm going out with my girlfriend. He says that's OK, she can come as well and we can rip up plants in the new council flowerbed.

'Hey, boys, come and look at Chett's cake now he's fixed it up.'

On the other side of the car park, Terry's coming out of the kitchen with Chett, who's holding a wedding cake with fancy icing and a little bride and groom on top. Terry's beaming.

'Little beaudy! Look at it! I'm getting him to take it in the shop to show Granny. Jeez, Chett mate, I don't know how you do it. Reckon you'll get full marks for this one.'

There's a low growl next to me. Suddenly Dylan's got me in a headlock. He twists my nose like it's the volume button on the stereo and snarls evilly, 'After work, let's chuck his cake in the river.'

I could hammer him. My nose is killing me. What's wrong with Dylan? Why's he got this thing about Chett? And then I see where he's looking. At Terry, laughing with Chett and slapping him on the back. And now I have it.

Dylan is not only lonely.

Dylan is jealous.

You have to feel sorry for him. He's actually frothing at the mouth with jealousy, although that could just be the tongue stud.

Luckily, at that moment Terry calls him over to admire the cake. I make my escape to the cold room to find Price and Boges leaning against the wall outside. Price is groaning in agony. He made himself look a complete moron in front of The Folders on his way to work. They asked him the time, and he did his impersonation of two Formula One cars losing control on a bend. Bogle's going to check out hypnotism.

By now, Terry and Dylan are taking delivery of several cardboard boxes from a Pocky uncle with a ute. Terry calls us over to help unpack them. He explains that the boxes contain firefighting equipment, which the park has to have by law.

He pats the pump proudly. 'It's a Goliath 263 Mark V. Four horsepower. Point that at your chimney and it'll lift the begga off.' Terry explains that firefighting is about water pressure and that, at its top setting, the Goliath can send water thirty-five metres in the air.

He asks me not to mention this to Clint and Cunningham.

After Terry's left to do his emails, Dylan suggests we carve rude drawings on the bus shelter with his set of chisels. I mutter, 'Cool! Whoa! Extreme!' and other Dylan-type language, then say I've got to help in the kitchen and hurry off. Just as I'm passing the farmhouse, I see Chett in the distance hitting the Dylan doll with the meat cleaver.

Terry calls me over to the farmhouse to say that he's going great with spellcheck. He tells me about Mrs McClaren's latest brainwave. It's really going to impress the Yarradindi Business Association.

The idea is that the Pockys start up a special fund called 'The Pocky Fund', using money from the Safari Park. This will go to deserving local charities, or people in need.

Terry's getting all the Pockys to think about deserving charities.

I feel like suggesting myself.

He heads off, then suddenly stops.

'Oh yeah, and Ian, bit of good news for you. Guess you're missing your girlfriend?'

I nod, puzzled.

He winks. 'She's coming here with her youth orchestra, Sat'd'y.' He beams. 'To play for the Business Association.'

I am dead. Buried. Cactus.

Tash is coming to the Pockys' on Saturday.

This is a total nightmare. This is the end of everything. I'll have to tell her I'm working here. I can't possibly get out of it if I'm a waiter. Or can I? Could I hide in the kitchen? That's impossible. Could I say I got the job just to see her? That's stupid. How incredible is that? I don't believe this, just as we're in sight of the end, everything's falling apart.

I slump against a shed. Terry chatters on. It was Mrs McClaren's idea – again. It will showcase local talent and prove to everyone how much the Pockys care about youth culture. Tash is going to play a special solo on the cello.

A solo on the cello? Then she's going to want her own cello! She'll ring Pilple and find out everything. But it's even worse. Because if her own cello's not ready *she'll have to play that lousy, squeaky school cello in front of the whole town!* I go all cold. She'll never forgive me. I mean, *never*.

Terry strolls off whistling. I'm sliding down the shed groaning as Bogle and Pricey rush up. I tell them. Bogle reckons the only way to do it is to pay Pilple to deliver the cello by Saturday lunchtime. He's instantly calculating.

'We owe the second payment of seven hundred and fifty dollars, minus the extra thirty you made last night from Mr Frye and your dad, so if you asked Pilple to deliver the cello here by Saturday lunchtime and said you'd pay him the rest then, PLUS an extra . . . fifty for doing it quicker, the sum you need now, on top of what we'll earn working full-time till then, bearing in mind the loss of half of Saturday's wages, is . . .'

We're staring at him in dread.

'. . . seventy dollars.'

We're done for. This is it. How are we going to find

another seventy bucks? We could ask Terry for a loan, but he'd tell Dad in microseconds.

At that moment Chett walks up and drags me aside.

'Dylan's 'air. Seventy bucks for another bit.'

17

We all gawp. This is spooky. How did he know we wanted exactly seventy dollars? Don't tell me he really is a witch. That's all we need. He's holding out some nail scissors. If I cut off any more of Mrs McClaren's hair she's going to look seriously bald. Maybe I can find a dog. A big golden retriever or something.

'I'll do it.'

He squints at me, grunts and slopes off.

Pricey's wide-eyed. 'Mate, you'll never get away with it a second time.'

'I won't cut McClaren's hair, I'll find a dog.' Bogle gives me a look.

'Even if you do, we've still got to get Pilple to fix the cello by Saturday lunchtime.' He folds his arms. 'Well, go on, ring him.'

I gulp and punch in Pilple's number. No answer.

'I'll have to ask him tonight when I pay him.'

Actually it's a reprieve – kind of. All I've got to do now is tell Tash I can't see her tomorrow night, make sure she doesn't go round to Piple's to see if she can get her cello for the Pocky concert – oh yes, and find a dog that'll let me chop off a chunk of its fur.

Piece of cake.

Not.

I get out my phone and text Tash: 'ps neighbr sez p bk sat morn I get cello to pckys sat noon 4 u 4 concert no prob love xxx'

I hit 'send' with a sense of doom.

Bogle blinks. 'Terrific. Now, my man, you gotta do it.'

Terry appears with our wages. I ask him about having Saturday morning's pay before the concert. He's fine about it. He can't wait to tell us the latest about the new Pocky charity. The money will be given to a scientist who's researching the endangered species and plants on Pocky land. All this person has to do is apply, explaining why they want the research money. Terry's already been up to the research camps to tell them. The handout will be called 'The Pocky Award for Nature, Trees and Science'.

Crusher's designing a wooden plaque for the winner. Being famous for doing ornamental lettering on wood by burning it in with a hot poker, he'll put 'The Pocky Award for Nature, Trees and Science' on it, along with the name of the winner.

Terry's going to present the award on Saturday, at the Yarradindi Business Association lunch.

He beams. 'Eh – guess who's gonna win.'

We shrug, trying to look interested. He glances

around, grins and whispers affectionately, 'Mr Frye. Can't wait to see his face.'

Neither can I.

'Mr Pocky. Any chance of overtime later?'

'Jeez, mate, you're keen as mustard! Meet me and Dyl at the footie ground at six. We gotta put up some Pockyloos.'

Bogle and Pricey go off on their bikes as Syd gives me a lift into town, telling me how the Pocky awards are going to get all the scientists onside so they don't tell the government about the disappearing tigers. It's weird to think of the Pockys handing out awards for nature. It's a bit like Attila the Hun giving prizes for citizenship.

I'm scouring the streets for golden retrievers and trying to think of an inoffensive way I can tell Tash I have to cancel our date tomorrow night. Getting her to talk to me would be a start.

At Pilple's, he watches gloomily as I count out the money. I'm just building up to ask him about getting the cello early, when he suddenly turns to me with that wild-eyed look and says, 'This girlfriend of yours. You seem pretty committed.'

'Er. Yeah.'

'My wife left me.'

'Oh.'

Right. Too much information, but at least it's broken the ice.

'Funny you should talk about me and my girlfriend,

Mr Pilple, because, er, she really needs that cello by Saturday lunchtime and I wondered, if we paid you another fifty dollars, whether you'd be able to get it done in time and drop it off at the Pockys' place by twelve midday and . . .'

Bad move. He's glaring at me with a weird, intense frown.

'You'd pay me an extra fifty dollars, just to please your girlfriend?'

I nod, checking the exits.

He frowns more deeply, stares at me for a long moment, then says briskly, 'All right. I'll drop it off at midday.'

Yes! I jog off. Piple's so weird. One minute he's savage, the next he's all sweetness and light. But who's complaining? I'm back in business. As of Saturday midday, Tash and me'll be OK again. She'll prob'ly even laugh. The next problem is finding a dog before six o'clock, when I've got to be at the sports ground to help with Pockyloos.

Right. Operation Fido. I head for the park. No dogs. I go down alleys. No dogs. Not only are there no golden retrievers, there are no four-legged animals at all. Where are they all? I'm starting to panic. Time is ticking away and I can't miss out on Terry's overtime. I see a woman with two sausage dogs and a man with an alsation. Now I'm peering over back fences. I hear some barking from a back garden and start creeping up a driveway. An old lady suddenly yells at me from a next-door window. I jump out of my skin and pelt down the street. In desperation, I head for the council dog pound. Not that I know what I'm going to say to them.

'Excuse me, my name's Ian Rude. Have you got a golden retriever handy so I can scalp it?'

It's all McClaren's fault. If she hadn't suggested the concert I wouldn't need Chett's seventy dollars. Now I end up trying to protect her stupid hair and . . .

'Hel-lo, Ian! You're just the person I wanted to see . . .'

It's her! It's Mrs McClaren! Leading the French kids out of our local museum. This is incredible. This is seriously strange. It's like fate is pushing me to chop her hair off. The French kid who saw me clip the first bit starts waving and doing victory signs behind her back.

'Now, Ian . . .' she turns her head towards the French kids and I see the hole, 'you're a native English speaker.' She smiles patronizingly. 'Have you ever thought about the different pronunciations of "o-u-g-h"? *Dough, through, cough, thorough, enough, bough, thought*?'

That's it. She's so irritating she deserves all her hair chopped off. As she looks round at the French kids I whip out the scissors and chop another bit of hair off the back. You can't say I didn't try.

The French kids go into hysterics. Mrs McClaren's completely bewildered. I rush off down the street. On the bright side, at least she's not hospitalized with mysterious meat-cleaver dents in her head. When I'm safely down the shopping mall, I ring Chett. Five minutes later the battered Monaro comes blasting up and screeches to a halt. He takes the hair, inspects it and hands over the seventy dollars.

Just as he's getting back in the car, he stops and grunts, 'Eh. I heard about ya deckin' Dylan. From now on, you and me . . .' he lifts a clenched fist in salute, 'Respect.'

Terrific. Respect from the neighbourhood warlock.

At the football ground, Terry and Dylan are already unloading five Pockyloos painted in team colours. Troy and a bunch of primary Pockys are swinging from the goalposts, kicking each other.

Terry beams at me. 'Ow ya goin', Ian! You and Dyl set these up while I take the little fellas inta see Troy's kindie teacher.' He lowers his voice. 'Caught him reading a book when he was s'posed to be doin' his Tae Kwan Do practice. It's only a phase but, well, the teacher should know about it.'

As soon as they roar off Dylan turns to me, grins wildly and says, 'Look over there.'

I hesitate. When a Pocky says this it's usually microseconds before a punch in the kidneys.

I notice he's got his hand in his pocket.

'Sucked in!'

A hail of big black hairy spiders suddenly flies up in my face. Dylan's whooping with pleasure. I yell and fight them off. They're fakes, of course. They're made out of fluffy black stuff and joined together by black cord. They're like some kind of Goth Christmas tree decoration. He pulls out another string of them.

'This is your one. Let's get someone!'

'What about The Pockyloos?'

'Quick, there's the mayor! Hide behind them trees, then jump out and shove 'em in his face.'

'No, no! Not him.'

'Who then?'

'Yo, Dyl!' I pretend I'm suddenly in need of a wrestle and jump him, bundling him off in the opposite direction from the mayor. We stagger round the corner as he hammers my head.

'Grannies! Get 'em!'

'No! No, Dylan!' I wrestle him away from a crowd of old ladies waiting for the community bus.

He breaks free and goes hurtling up to the bandstand to rip off a dangling poster. I rush after him.

Suddenly my phone rings. It's Tash. My heart flips inside me. *Tash!*

'Tashie, hi!'

'Ian, can we talk? Look, about what happened at Bree's place . . .'

I'm over the moon to hear her voice but Dylan's doing sign language to me about a group of American tourists coming up the street. The idea seems to be that we lasso them with the spiders, then thump them.

Tash is saying, 'The thing is, I got really upset when

you said you didn't want Bree's *Cemetery Trashers* and . . .'

I'm desperate to talk to her, but there's no way I can do it with Dylan going ballistic in the background.

I cut in. 'Tash, look, I can't talk. Stuff's happening here . . .'

'What stuff? Where are you?'

I can't tell her I'm with Dylan Pocky.

Now he's running at me, laughing insanely. He's going to jump me.

I gabble, 'I'm helping my dad with the lino stripping. See you outside Joey's in ten minutes! Aaargh . . .'

Dylan pounces, whooping. My phone flies out of my hand. He's got me pinned against a wall. He's trying to stuff the spiders down the back of my T-shirt.

From out of nowhere come Ruby and about eight Folders. Dylan sights them, bellows like an ape, rushes up to Ruby and starts stuffing the spiders down *her* back. The Folders are yelling and bashing him. Where's my phone? The Folders start bashing me as well.

'No! Stop! Ouch!'

Ruby sees the rope of spiders hanging out of my pocket, grabs it and tries to shove it down *my* back.

I grab her wrists and try to wrestle her off. She's shrieking with laughter. They're all laughing. Ruby's grinning face is jammed into mine.

Around the corner walks . . . Tash.

18

She gasps. It looks like I'm in a clinch with Ruby.

'No. Tash, you don't understand!'

She's all red. 'I totally understand. I totally understand. Home helping your dad, are you? Liar!'

The Folders shriek with laughter. 'Hey, Natasha, want a spider?'

Tash storms off, furious and humiliated.

'Tash!'

Three Folders suddenly hurl themselves at me, shove me against a wall and start thumping me, laughing. I'm desperate to run after Tash but, as fast as I get rid of one, another pounces. Dylan's hooting with laughter. I'm yelling furiously at them to stop, but they think that's even funnier.

I finally wrench free and belt towards Joey's.

Why was she here?

What have I done? Stupid Ruby. Stupid Dylan.

Stupid, stupid me.

I rush into Joey's quad. Where is she?

And then I see her. Right over the other side of the quad. She's standing in an archway with Günter and they're up close talking. They're more than close. They're staring into each other's eyes. And as I look, she leans forward – and squeezes his arm. My stomach backflips.

'Tash!' I run towards her, yelling out her name. She's ignoring me, walking off with Günter.

'Tash! Tash!'

I pound across the quad.

'Hey, what are you doing?' It's a teacher.

'I'm here to see someone, sir.'

'Well, you can't. This is music-programme students only.'

'Please. I have to. It's urgent.'

'No you don't. Out. Out.'

This is pointless. Tash is gone anyway. I hurry out of the gates and reach frantically for my phone.

I've lost my phone.

I fly back to the spot where I dropped it, fighting off Dylan. It's not there, and there's no trace of Dylan or Ruby or any of them. I hunt everywhere. I sink down on to a bench. I can't believe this. After everything else that's happened, I've lost my mobile. I can't contact Tash, she can't contact me, she thinks I'm on with Ruby Pearson, so she's prob'ly going out with Günter. Oh yes – and when they hear about the mobile my parents are going to kill me.

I'd try to find a public phone, but they're all smashed. I stumble off, my head spinning. If Tash phones or texts me, nobody will reply, and she'll think

I'm deliberately cutting her. Even worse, Dylan or one of The Folders might reply.

My chest grabs.

I'll have to ring her from home – not what I want to do, since our home phone is so public. This is one call I don't want overheard.

When I get home, Dad's standing right next to the phone showing Mum the half-finished sanding. Apart from a few major grooves, it looks reasonable. Dad says Terry's organizing a special cut price on what's supposed to be the best varnish. Mum says she hopes the varnish isn't foreign.

Daisy gives me a huge grin, puts her arms out to me for a cuddle and says, 'Wee-an.' I take her. She hugs me tight, round my neck. I could cry. I don't.

Mum asks after Tash and I try to act casual.

I help Dad clear up for four dollars, waiting for a chance to get to the phone. There isn't one. Finally I give up and flop into bed. I'll borrow Bogle's phone tomorrow. I'll tell her *everything*. I've got to get her back from Günter.

I've got to *fix* things.

Next morning there's no chance to get to our phone. As The Tysonmobile bounces along towards the Safari Park, Syd's strangely worried. He whispers that last night when he went back in his boat to put down more sausages he bumped right into Mr Frye.

Syd, of course, thinks he was there doing scientific research. I immediately realize Frye was spying on him. Syd tells me how they had this weird conversation and Mr Frye kept asking what was in the bag, and Syd kept having to pretend he didn't hear. It ended up with Syd having to go home without putting down any more sausages. Apparently, Mr Frye stood watching him all the way back across the swamp. I hope old Frye's not on to him. If the Parks and Wildlife people find out about the sausages, the Pockys will be in deep trouble. For the first time it occurs to me – so will I.

That's all I need.

Syd's big worry is that if all the sausages have been eaten and not replaced, the tigers won't come, and now it's too risky to put out more.

As we pull into the car park, Dylan's yelling and holding up something. Oh, excellent. He's got my phone!

'Yo, Rudie! You dropped your phone.'

The last thing to do is look too interested.

I drawl, 'Thangs, made. I'll be rye-dover . . .' and stroll across as casually as I can.

He's jigging on the spot.

'Yo-ho, Rudie, guess what, that girl texted ya. She's ropeable. She's totally dissing you, man. So guess what?' He chortles. 'I texted back.'

My blood runs cold.

'What did she text you, Dylan?'

'I dunno. I deleted it.'

'What did you text back?'

He gives his high-pitched snorty laugh. 'I done –

get this – "Get nicked, fat butt"!' He crows with laughter.

I'm turned to stone. I can't breathe. I could kill him but there's no time for that. Tash! I stumble off in a flat panic and call her number. I get voicemail.

'Tash, Dylan stole my phone. That wasn't me. I swear to you. This is all a total mistake.'

Dylan runs up behind me and snatches the phone.

'Get nicked, ya dumb chick . . .'

I wrestle him for it. He roars with laughter. He's got no idea of what he's done. He thinks this is all a big joke. I'm punching and clawing at him.

A voice says, 'Now, boys, that's quite enough rough-housing . . .'

It's Mrs McClaren, with Terry in tow.

I yell, 'He took my phone!'

Dylan whoops, 'Na, it's my phone, miss. He took it . . .'

'Well, if you can't resolve your problem without violence, then there's only one answer, isn't there?' She beams around. 'We remove the source of the problem until the end of the day, when I hope you both will have come back to your senses.'

Don't take my phone, you idiotic old bat!

Terry's awkward. 'But . . . it's Ian's phone, isn't it?'

She cuts him off triumphantly. 'That's not the point Mr Pocky. The point is that the trick to controlling teenagers is not permitting your children to make you take sides. It's called "taking the wind out of their sails" . . .'

At the mention of wind, Dylan instantly does an armfart. This is insane.

I'm spluttering. 'But, Mr Pocky, it's my phone! Honestly! It's my phone!'

For one wonderful moment I think he'll see sense, but Mrs McClaren raises an eyebrow at him.

He coughs and mutters awkwardly, 'Come on, Dyl mate, hand it over . . .'

I feel my jaw drop open. *This can't happen.*

Dylan beams at the attention from Terry. Like a lamb, he hands my mobile to Mrs McClaren, who smiles victoriously and drops it into her handbag.

'All aborra Tysonmobile a tour a tigers, a cheeky beggas!' I hurry across to Syd. I could kill McClaren. How can she do this to me? I didn't think it was possible things could get worse with Tash, but now, this! We're completely out of contact. In the distance, Clint Pocky and Cunningham come pelting out of the shower block. Two seconds later, one of the scientists, his face covered in shaving cream, rushes out after them, shouting about Clint shutting off the hot water.

We're off on the tour. And Syd's right, there are no tigers at all. We go so far into the bush that the track runs out. I do my best with the commentary, but my mind's on Tash. I've got to get Bogle's mobile and call her. No, forget that. I can't do something as touchy as this by phone. I've got to go to Joey's and tell her – tell her everything to her face and hope to high heaven that she believes me.

Of all the things Dylan could have called her. I get a flashback to her face in that dress shop when I said her bum was big. I could die.

As The Tysonmobile draws into the car park Syd's going on and on about the lack of tigers. I'm desperately running through what I'll say to Tash. But Terry's pelting across from the farmhouse, waving a sheet of paper. He bangs wildly on The Tysonmobile door. Syd opens it.

Terry's white-faced.

'Ian, quick, come to the office.'

Not now, I've got to get to Tash. 'I can't, Mr Pocky.'

'You gotta. Something shockin' with the computer . . .'

'Find Bogle, I've got to get into town.'

I'm desperate.

He's dragging me along.

I'll drive you into town later. You gotta help.'

As he hurries me in through the back door of the office, I catch a glimpse of Granny at the front door trying to reason with Mr Frye, who's going bananas. I duck behind Terry so he doesn't see me. Crowds of Pockys are flooding up from every direction. What about Tash?

'Mr Pocky, I've really got to get back into town . . .'

But Terry's staring at me, his eyes wide with shock. 'Ian, mate, the computer.' He gulps. 'We got a smacker.'

19

'A smacker?'

'A smacker.'

'You don't mean a hacker?'

'Hacker, smacker. They've changed me email to Mr Frye about the Science award.'

He shows me the sheet of paper. His hand is shaking.

'This is what I wanted to send Mr Frye. Done it all proper, then typed it out . . .'

In Terry's handwriting it reads:

Dear Mr Fry,

The Pocky family are doneting The Pocky Award for Nature, Trees and Sceience to sceientists, and we want you to be the first. We know you are on a Budgit so we have passed round the hat because we don't want to see you walking round the bush doing sceientific research without The Pocky Award for Nature, Trees and Sceience anymore so write a letter to Mrs Maclerin straightaway saying you need The Pocky Award for

Nature, Trees and Sceience and the Pockys are right
behind you you little ripper
   Your friends
   The Pocky family

His voice is shaking. 'And look what come out on the computer. Mr Frye just brought it round.'

I read.

Dear Mr Fry,

   The Picky family are donating pants to scientists, and we want you to be the first. We know you are on a budget so we have passed round the hat because we don't want to see you walking round the bush doing scientific research without pants anymore so write a letter to Mrs Malaren straightaway saying you need pants and the Pockys are right behind you little ripper

   Your friends
   The Picky family

This is insane. This is a nightmare. Tash thinks we're over and I'm trapped discussing underpants with Terry Pocky.

'Mr Pocky, did you use autotext and spellcheck?'

'Course I did. Done the initials of the Pocky Award, like you told me.'

I type 'pnts', and hit autotext. It comes out as 'The

Pocky Award for Nature, Trees and Science'. What's he done wrong?

I suddenly realize. I type 'pnts', ignore the autotext prompt and hit spellcheck instead. It comes out as 'pants'. That's it. He's typed 'pnts', ignored the auto-text prompt, then accepted all the spellcheck changes without looking at what they were.

How do I explain? I gabble, 'You used spellcheck *instead* of autotext. So the computer asked you if "pnts" meant "pants" and you said yes.'

His jaw drops. 'I never! I never said I meant pants, I—'

I interrupt, 'No, no, the computer did it.'

'The computer wrote about people's underpants?'

'It asked you and you accepted it.'

'The computer asked me to write about under-pants? On its own?'

'That's what spellcheck does.'

'You told me it done your spelling.'

'It does. But when it does, it suggests changes to what you've written and you have to say yes or no . . .'

'The computer makes changes to your letters? The computer starts making rude suggestions? Just ups and writes stuff about underpants all by itself? We gotta take it back.'

'But—'

'Who else has it bin writing to? It coulda written to all me friends.'

'It can only send emails to people when you tell it to.'

I stare at him.

Oh no . . .

'You didn't send any other emails, did you?'

'Only to the Yarradindi Business Association.'

We're staring in horror at Terry's email.

Dear Member of the Yarradindi Business Association

Give your own pants to scientists

The Picky family are proud to announce that it is handing out pants to Mr Fry and other scientists. Would you like to donate your own pants? It will only cost you a couple of hundred dollars, and Mr Fry and his mates are desperate. You can donate your pants anonymously, or you can have them named after you. For example, the Yarradindi Ladies' Bowling Club has already decided to give their pants for Botany. Don't miss the chance to be the first in your trade to donate your own pants. Your name will be engraved with a hot poker.

Thanking you,

The Picky Family.

Terry's mouth is hanging open.

'You told me it done your spelling! You told me it done your spelling . . . !'

Mr Frye bursts in, yelling, followed by Granny and Syd, still trying to calm him down.

'How dare you suggest I walk round the wilderness area without underpants! How dare you suggest I need people to give me their old underwear . . .'

'I never! It was the computer! Ian'll tell you . . .'

I stammer, 'He's right. He got confused between spellcheck and autotext. Mr Frye, about me being here—'

But he's not interested in me at all.

He cuts in. 'Not content with deliberately smashing up my garden with a water tank—'

'I swear that was an accident . . .'

'What about your brother plucking twelve chickens in a high wind the same day I painted my shed?'

'That's Crush. He was in a daydream. He didn't realize all them feathers'd get stuck to it . . .'

'I am past explanations. I am standing up for what I think is right. Don't think I don't know what you're up to. Don't think I'm going to stand by and let you wipe out those tigers.'

Terry's appalled. 'We're not wiping out the tigers . . .'

'Oh really? Then what's this?'

Mr Frye rummages in his pocket, pulls out a crumpled handkerchief and opens it. Inside, covered in dirt, is one of the sausages Syd and I buried. In the background, Syd's face is twisted up with anxiety. He suddenly hurries out. I don't blame him. Meanwhile, Terry's looking at the sausage, mystified.

'A sausage?'

'Yes. A sausage deliberately set as bait for the tigers. Unless . . .' Frye sneers, 'you were planning to grow a sausage tree.'

Terry's eyebrows shoot up, then sink into a puzzled frown. He's obviously deciding that Frye is a complete lunatic.

He says, gently, 'No, mate. See, sausages don't come from trees, they come from animals . . .'

Frye gives a strangled yelp of rage. 'I know sausages don't grow on trees, you moron! This sausage was deliberately buried to trap the tigers and kill them, so you can turn them into more tigerskin rugs and cushions like the ones you've got in your so-called "museum" . . .'

Terry's amazed. 'No way. Gimme a look at that . . .'

'Don't you threaten me. I'll have the police on to you for assault.'

'For tryna to look at a sausage?'

An unmistakable voice rises over the escalating row. 'Gentlemen, I'm sure there's a sensible explanation.'

Mrs McClaren is elbowing her way through the Pockys. How does she do it? She must have a special disaster-sensing device.

Frye turns to her with blazing eyes and jabs a finger at Terry.

'They are trying to destroy the tigers.'

'We're not! 'Ow we destroying the tigers? We're tryna give out an award for scientific research . . .'

Terry tells Mrs McClaren that the computer has gone mad and is sending out obscene letters.

Mr Frye rages about suing Terry for suggesting that he runs round the bush without his underpants. Luckily, he's so furious you can't make out what he's trying to say about the sausages. I'm trying to explain but no one will listen.

Granny says she's not having a sex-maniac computer in the house. She reckons it might be looking up her skirt and transmitting the findings to the neighbourhood.

Crusher comes in with a tray of cream buns to calm everyone down. Mr Frye tells him he knows what he can do with his buns. Terry keeps telling Frye he's sorry and that he's going to put a bar on the computer until it's sorted and he knows nothing about buried sausages.

But Mr Frye storms and threatens. Mrs McClaren takes me aside.

'Ian, we have to defuse this. You take Mr Frye back to his property and get him a cup of tea. I'll look after Mr Pocky.'

'But I have to go into town.'

'Civic responsibility is more important than our own petty concerns, Ian.'

This is crazy. I've got to get to Tash. Mrs McClaren brings the whole yelling mob to silence. 'Mr Pocky, do you agree to send an apology to everyone who got those emails?'

'Too right, Mrs Mac. What's more, I'll do what we done with the phone when the kids kept ringing long distance. I'll put a bar on the computer so no one can email Mr Frye.'

Frye explodes that there's no such thing as a computer bar. I coax him away, checking my watch. If I'm lucky I can get him home and still catch Tash at the end of her lunch hour. Meanwhile, Frye's raging. He says the Pockys haven't heard the last of this. I'm racking my brains for ways to calm him down as fast as possible so I can get away.

I make him a cup of tea and suggest we see if Terry's sent out the apology email. I get online. There's a message from Terry entitled: 'Apology'.

'There you are, Mr Frye, it's already gone out to the whole town.'

Thank heavens for that. At least that should help a bit. Mr Frye sits down, breathing heavily. We open it.

Dear Friend,
    Our computer just sent Mr Fry a rude letter so we are putting a bra on him.
    Thanking you
    The Picky family

20

Frye lets out a rising roar of fury.

'Tell me that's not a calculated insult. Well, the Pockys will get their comeuppance. You know, Ian, the only thing that keeps me going is the knowledge that, out there, there are young fighters for the planet like you.' He claps me on the shoulder. 'I will never forget the initiative you've shown in getting yourself a job with the Pockys so you can find out exactly what they're up to.'

Eh?

He's staring at me with that insane look of his. 'I am going to trust you with vital information.'

Oh no.

He leads me through the kitchen, past a cage of convalescing bats, off towards some dense bush at the edge of his land. He's rattling on.

'The tigers are clearly suffering a serious dietary imbalance, doubtless due to the food being put down by the Pockys. Their coats are lifeless, they are covered in fleas and they are obviously depressed.'

We slog through some bushland and come to a

marshy bit where his land meets the end of the Pocky swamp.

He grins. 'See that finger of land? That's one of my boundaries with the Pockys. It's a natural bridge across the wetlands. Follow me.' He veers to the left and into some dense trees. Suddenly we come to a wide, fenced clearing.

Right in the middle of the clearing are pens and – I don't believe this – a big bunch of skinny tigers. My jaw drops. Mr Frye has been rustling the tigers. His face is shining with pride.

'You are the only person apart from me who knows this. Not even Natasha knows it, for her own protection. This, Ian, is the world's only captive breeding programme for the South-east Australian Thylacine.' He leans down to me, his eyes glowing. 'In the absence of any sensible help from the Parks and Wildlife Department, *I* am saving the tigers. I can't let them be wiped out. Inside this sanctuary I already have twelve adult tigers and five cubs, all of which are learning to hunt for food and not to rely on humans. The tigers will be saved for your children, Ian. And your children's children.'

So that's what happened to the tigers. Mr Frye explains he's been trapping them for the last two months and bringing them back across the land bridge. He nabbed another two last night. 'You can go now. And Ian . . .' he puts out his hand and shakes mine, 'this is our secret.'

Not another one!

I run off. The man's demented. And the Pockys are in big trouble because if Frye's capturing all the tigers, there won't be any left to make an appearance on the safari tours, sausages or no sausages. But it's Tash I need to worry about. If I'm lucky I can still get The Tysonmobile back into town and catch her in her lunch break.

Syd drops me outside Joey's. Tash is nowhere to be seen. I spot Bree.

'Hi, Bree, d'you know where Tash is?'

She looks at the ground, embarrassed.

I start to panic. 'Bree? Where's Tash?'

'Sorry, Ian, but she said to say . . .' She tails off.

'What?'

'She said, if you turned up, to say . . . she doesn't want to see you any more.'

Everything stops. I stare at Bree and hear myself give a choked gasp. I stumble off. A mob of kids yells out, 'Yo, pissycarto!' I'm out of Joey's and striding blindly down the street. My mind's racing. How can I explain to her? How can I get her back? I stop in my tracks.

That's it.

The Yarradindi Business Association lunch. She can't avoid me there. I'm still in with a chance.

I stride into the station forecourt and see instantly that something is very wrong. Syd's next to The Tysonmobile, twitching with anxiety, and propped next to one of the front tyres is a large sign reading: 'Tiger Tour cancelled'.

'Quick, gerra board, a terrible business a Safari Park . . .'

'What's happened?'

'Lunch a cancelled. Yarradindi Business Association angry arra emails, not coming a Sat'dy, a silly beggas, Terry a state, mayor ouda Safari Park telling him off, aaah. Dunno warra do, poor Terry aaah.'

My heart sinks. The lunch is my last chance to see Tash properly until the music camp is over. If I have to wait till *then*, she'll definitely be dating Günter.

Syd rattles on. I listen hopelessly as we roar along. Apparently, Terry's emails have caused an uproar all over town. The committee of the Yarradindi Business Association has voted to have nothing more to do with the Pockys whatsoever. The mayor has actually driven out to the Safari Park to deliver a written letter of protest. Terry's chances of getting voted into the Yarradindi Business Association are zilch.

As we pull into the car park a mob of anxious Pockys plus a crowd of curious tourists is milling round outside the Pocky farmhouse. The mayor's shouts echo from inside. I jump out and jostle my way through the crowd. The mayor is saying, 'It was not only the Yarradindi Ladies' Bowling Club that you insulted, you repeatedly insulted Mr Frye.'

Terry's saying pathetically, 'I never!'

'Hel-lo, everyone, now let's all stop arguing, because I think we have a solution.'

It's Mrs McClaren, of course – but now she's with Frye, of all people. And, strangely, he's not furious. In fact, he's smiling.

Mrs McClaren holds up her hand for silence.

'Ladies and gentlemen and the Pocky family, I have just had a call from Mrs Peters, the chairperson of the Yarradindi Ladies' Bowling Club. The ladies are pre-pared to accept Mr Pocky's explanation and apology.'

The Pockys break into applause.

'And I am delighted to say that Mr Frye has also accepted Mr Pocky's explanation and apology.'

The Pockys applaud even more.

Mrs McClaren silences them again.

'Furthermore,' she pauses dramatically, 'Mr Frye has just told me that he would be very happy to accept the first Pocky Award for Nature, Trees and Science at the lunch tomorrow, as long as the Yarradindi Business Association is there in full force to hear his acceptance speech!'

Frye accepting the award? I don't like that at all. What's he up to? But the Pockys explode into whistles and whoops. The mayor scowls and heads off in his Merc. Terry's patting me on the back, saying I was a big help. Granny hugs me, and I catch a glimpse of the croc rolling in the wrinkles. Crusher gives me a high-five and nearly knocks me over.

At least the lunch is on and I'll have a fighting chance to talk Tash round.

Syd's at my elbow, looking anxious. 'Quick, gorra talka you a Tysonmobile a plan B, aaah, a clever begga.'

He hurries me off past the car park towards a gigantic old shed at the end of a paddock. He unlocks its doors. Inside is The Tysonmobile. What's it doing here?

'Aaaah a cheeky begga sniffa bus aaah!'

'What?'

'Sniffa! Sniffa wheels! Sniffa, quicka silly begga!'

'Sniff it?'

There's a lot of anxious gargling. I lean down and sniff. Nothing.

'Lower!'

I lean down lower. There's a familiar warm smell.

'Is it . . . sausage?'

'Shhh! But carra smell higher up?'

'No, you can only smell it right down here.'

Syd sighs with relief and quickly explains that he's just smeared the tyres and mudguards of The Tysonmobile with raw mashed-up sausages left over from the batch that had to be junked because of Crusher's armpits. It's a last-ditch effort to get the tigers to show up during the Business Association tour tomorrow. He can't plant any more sausages in case Mr Frye sees him doing it. So, instead, he's going to take the sausage-smeared Tysonmobile into tiger territory at midnight, and do circuits of the entire area. That way the tigers will get the smell of sausages and, with a bit of luck, tomorrow they'll turn up in big numbers.

Mr Frye isn't likely to be there and, if he is, Syd can just say he's checking out a new safari route.

How can I tell him that Frye could well be there, but the tigers won't?

'Knowa tigers. Nevaresist a Pocky beer and Vegemite sausage, a cheeky beggas.'

I try to fudge my way through it. 'But, Mr Pocky, feeding the tigers is against the law . . .'

Not that there're going to be any tigers . . .

Syd gives a panicked laugh.

'Norraginst a law a give a *smell* a starvin' beggas.'

21

Syd explains that, technically, at no point will anybody be feeding the tigers because The Tysonmobile will never stop in one place long enough for the tigers even to get a lick. 'Mr Pocky, if anyone smells it, you'll be in deep trouble.'

Syd nods in agreement, stares at me with despairing eyes and whispers hoarsely, 'Aaaah, after email aborra Pocky awards a only chance.'

'Won't it wash off when you go across the swamp?'

'Naa, fullagrease a Pocky sausages. Eighty per cent. Gorra do it, Ian.' He sighs. 'Young Terry – don't get inna Business Association, a break 'is 'eart.'

He claps me on the shoulder.

'You help me? You with me, a cheeky begga?'

I sigh. But I can't look into Syd's desperate eyes and tell him all this won't change a thing.

'With you, Syd.'

He beams. 'Good boy, Ian. Allus rely on Ian.'

I feel terrible.

As we head back to the main buildings, Syd fills me

in on the plan for tomorrow. There won't be any tours for the general public, only one for the Yarradindi Business Association people, after their lunch. At about eleven thirty, Syd will pretend he and I are going to clean The Tysonmobile. Really, we'll be taking The Tysonmobile into the big shed to re-smear it with sausage meat so the smell is fresh and strong.

Syd grins conspiratorially. 'Nerra tella Terry. Go madda silly begga, aaah!'

Around us there's a frenzy of happy Pocky activity. Terry's hammering up a big sign. It reads: 'Welcome to the Yarradindi Business Association' and 'You're not a freako just because you love the eco'.

Under Granny's supervision, Clint, Cunningham, Troy and the primary Pockys are tidying up. Bogle is weeding a flower bed while Pricey cleans the pen of Bruce Willis, the emu. On the far side of the paddock is Chett. He's got a new Dylan doll with a bigger bit of Mrs McClaren's hair stuck to it. He's stabbing it with a fork.

As I walk past Dylan an electric shock zaps my arm. He whoops triumphantly, holds up a little metal thing and sniggers. 'Godoffa electric cooker!'

I search everywhere for Mrs McClaren to get my phone back in case Tash rings, but she's already gone home. I don't dare ring Tash myself, of course. Brilliant. A week ago I had the best relationship in the world. Now I'm fighting not to lose her.

Crusher gives us our instructions for waiting on

tables tomorrow. Bogle, Pricey, Dylan and me have to wear white shirts and school pullovers, so we look like real waiters. Along with Syd, our job is to hand out prawn cocktails and plates of sausages cooked by Crusher, then spoon on to each a serving of peas and a scoop of mash. Chett will be preparing the prawn cocktails, peas and mash in the little kitchen next to the cold room for us to collect from him and take to the marquee. He'll have to do it all by himself, so Granny and the other elderly Pockys can have the main kitchen to serve the regular tourists in the cafe. Tash's orchestra is arriving at twelve o'clock. They'll play for the lunch, then, while the Yarradindi Business Association goes off on the tour, they'll set up their music stands on a stage on the lawn, because the Pocky Award Ceremony is going to be open to the public. Chairs for the audience will be set in front on a gigantic groundsheet. As the grand finale to the Award Ceremony, Tash will play her solo.

This is all fitting into place. It just about gives me time to do the sausage smearing, get the cello from Pilple and explain everything to Tash before the lunch gets started. By five past twelve tomorrow all my problems will be over.

I hope.

We spend the rest of the evening painting the town crest on The Pockyloos, plus the words: 'Don't panic, we're organic'.

I fill Bogle and Pricey in on everything that's

happened. Pricey's jaw drops. Bogle just slowly shakes his head.

At ten o'clock Terry gives me a lift home, since he needs to drop off the can of cut-price varnish for our floor. Dad takes it, doing a spectacular leap to put it on a shelf in our garage.

Terry beams expansively, 'Ya know, Pete. Mrs Mac reckons I might even end up seccatary of the Business Association,' and adds that this, as everybody knows, is only a hair's breadth away from being mayor.

I crawl into bed drained.

Tomorrow's the day.

In the morning I'm up before six and ready and waiting for Syd, who turns up in the empty Tysonmobile, reserved today exclusively for the Business Association tour. He looks exhausted. He's only had three hours' sleep after driving The Tysonmobile round and round the tigers' territory. 'Aaah, never saw a single tiger, a sneaky beggas.' He stares at me red-eyed. 'We gorra see 'em today, Ian. We gorra.'

I smile feebly. Because, of course, we won't.

It's already sweltering. The Safari Park is bustling with Pockys still scrubbing, mowing and weeding. Granny's reversing a big truck on to the paddock facing the rainforest. On the back is the giant tent that Crusher borrowed from mates in the circus industry. Syd and I go over to help unload and put it up. The man I'm working next to explains that normally he's the legs of a human pyramid.

We hold the ladder as Terry runs an electric cable from the tent to the overhead powerlines, so Crusher can install fans inside for the guests. I ask if that isn't a bit dangerous. Terry explains that yeah, touch that cable and you get six billion volts through you. But I'm not to worry because he's looping the cable very safely on the roof of the marquee, and in the trade it's what's known, technically, as a safe risk.

By the time we've done that it's eight thirty, and outside the museum a mob of Pocky aunties is being drilled by Crusher as guides. They're wearing identical blouses and badges that read: 'Help Im a Pocky'. Bruce Willis the emu is bobbing his head at them over the fence. Noddy the vicious kangaroo tries to maul Auntie Barbara.

Eight forty-five. Every time I think of Tash arriving, I get butterflies.

'Tash, the reason I've been weird is because of the cello . . .'

Crusher rounds up Bogle, Pricey and me for breakfast. After that, we get put on kitchen duty. About fifteen Pockys are peeling potatoes, Chett in the middle of them. Crusher, red with sweat, is carting out the enormous barbie.

'Tash, when you saw me with Dylan and Ruby . . .'

Time's ticking down. It's nearly lunch. By now the tables and chairs are all set up. I get Pricey and Bogle and we whip off to get our wages from Terry. He beams, and gives us twenty dollars extra. I fly back to the kitchen because it's time for sausage smearing. Sure enough, Syd's already looking for me. He hurries me off to the big shed and locks the door behind us. From under a pile of sacking he drags out a big plastic bag of sausages.

'Rub overa tyres a mudguards, aaaah, a cheeky begga!'

There's five minutes before Pilple arrives. I grab a handful of sausages and start smearing. Bogle should be here. He'd love this. When it's done I pelt off to the car park. The Yarradindi Business Association people are milling about and – yes! – Pilple's arrived with the cello! I race up.

My heart's pounding. I open the case, hardly daring to look. But it's amazing. It's as good as new.

'That's brilliant, Mr Pilple! Fantastic!'

'I hope your girlfriend appreciates everything you've done.'

I feel a surge of panic. She can't appreciate it because she doesn't know about it. All she knows is that I've been behaving like I'm not interested in her.

He stares at me for a long moment and mutters, 'You really care about that girl, don't you . . . ?'

For an instant he rests a fatherly hand on my arm. *Eh?*

Just as suddenly, he's in his car and off. Bogle and Pricey rush up to see the cello. They beam!

Stoked!

At that very moment the bus with Tash and the rest of the orchestra pulls into the car park. They pour out and head into the marquee. I see Tash, and my stomach somersaults. This is it. I snap the cello case closed, run my hand through my hair to tidy myself up – and find myself face to face with Chett.

He grabs me by the collar. 'That 'air. You sure you got it from Dylan?'

'Course I did.'

'I done my biggest hex on him and it isn't working.'

'So when did you do it?'

'Just now.'

'Oh well, then . . . !' I'm desperately looking for Tash over his shoulder. 'Everyone knows that hexes only work when the earth's gravity's pulling in direct ratio to the biosphere.'

His eyebrows knit with bewilderment. I wriggle free and hurry into the orchestra tent with the cello. There she is! My face is nearly splitting with a smile.

'Tashie, I got your cello, I—'

She snatches it.

'I can't believe it – on top of everything else, you're working for the Pockys. Terry told me.'

'I can explain.'

'Explain to your friend Ruby.'

'She's not my friend.'

'Liar,' she spits out. 'Heidi saw you with her that

time you said you had to go home and work for your dad.'

I'm shocked by her savageness.

'But Tash, she's not . . . I'm not—'

Her eyes narrow. She cuts me off. 'I tried not to believe it, but then I saw it. With my *own eyes*.'

And she storms off into a pack of kids from the orchestra.

22

I just stand there, reeling. How can it be so difficult to explain?

Bogle's in front of me.

'Disaster. Ruby. She's come to the lunch with her dad. She's sitting on one of Price's tables.'

I'm already running. 'Tell Pricey to stick his head in a bucket of water. I've got to talk to Tash.'

But I can't talk to her, because just as I hurry into the big tent the orchestra starts playing. I swear under my breath. Mrs McClaren and Syd are herding in the Yarradindi Business Association. Crusher's anxiously turning fifty sausages on the barbecue.

I'll have to get her during a break. I snatch up a tray of prawn cocktails from the kitchen and quickly serve them out, trying to catch her eye. She's refusing to look at me but *definitely* glancing at Günter.

As I go out again, it's Frye, whispering hoarsely in my ear.

'Ian? Good that you're here. Today, at the cere-mony, I am going to expose the Pockys for what they are. Because, I have . . . this!' He holds up an envelope.

Don't tell me he's found out about the sausage meat on The Tysonmobile? There's no time to pump him, because Dylan and Price have both disappeared, and Crusher has me and Bogle running off our feet.

In the kitchen, Dylan's yelling insults at Chett, who's bellowing more back as he frantically dollops prawn-cocktail mix into bowls. His elbow catches a bowl. It tips and clips the one next to it. In slow motion, the whole lot go crashing to the floor. Dylan whoops, jumps feet first into the mess, grinds it round and runs out.

Chett's hysterical. 'There's no more prawns! What we gonna do?'

There's nothing else we can do. We scoop the gritty mess back in the bowls. Chett slops on more mayonnaise to cover the grit. Bogle dashes in to help us. We serve it up to the guests.

In the orchestra, Günter's smiling at Tash. The mayor and his mates are being nasty about the Pockys, so I give them the grittiest prawns. Now Bogle's scuttling up to me. 'Quick, Pricey's in trouble. Water's not working.'

Why do they always come to me?

Price is stumbling round outside the tent, his face a strawberry.

I march him into the cold room, rip open a bag of

166

peas and pour them into a bucket which I jam into his hands.

'Stick your face in that and pull yourself together.'

I'm going crazy not being able to clear things up with Tash.

Now Crusher's giving me bowls of sausages. Relief! The orchestra's stopped for a break. I dash outside.

'Tash, Ruby was stuffing Dylan Pocky's spiders down my neck. That other time I was selling her CDs . . .'

She's talking right over me. 'Yeah, your mate Dylan Pocky.' Tears spring into her eyes. ''S'pose you had a good laugh together discussing my big butt.'

'No! Dylan *stole* my phone, believe me.'

'Believe *you*?' she explodes. 'What reason have I had to do that?'

The teacher yells, 'Back to your places, orchestra.'

I punch my leg in frustration. Now Crusher's telling me to hand out more sausages. I'm desperately trying to catch Tash's eye.

And again, it's Bogle.

'Quick, Price has locked himself in the walk-in freezer.'

'Tell him to get nicked.'

Bogle raises his eyebrows. I snort with exasperation and pelt into the cold room.

'Price, come out – you'll kill yourself.'

'Not till I've stopped looking red.'

'I'll tell you if you're still red.'

'You won't.'

'I will.'

When he opens up, he's got blue lips, a face as red as a beetroot and peas in his hair. Now is not the time for truth.

'You're fine. Take out this bowl of mash.'

Granny, passing, gasps and tells him he should see a doctor about his sunburn.

The lunch continues in a blur. We're collecting dirty dishes, serving up meringues. Price gets redder and redder. Finally, Ruby looks over her coffee cup, bats her eyelashes and sneers, 'Pricey, something wrong with your face?'

We grab him a split second before he locks himself in the freezer. He's wrestling us to shut the door.

'I wanna die! I'm gonna die. I can't be *this red*!'

I snap. He thinks *he's* got problems?

I snatch up Dylan's electric zapper and jab it in Pricey's chest. 'OK. Aversion therapy. Think of Ruby.'

Zap!

'Ow!'

'Think of Ruby!'

Zap! Zap!

'Ow!'

Zap! Zap! Zap!

Bogle whispers, 'That's not gonna work.'

I put a finger to my lips. 'All in the mind. You right, Price?'

Price blinks and nods uncertainly. I shove a plate of after-dinner mints into his hands and hustle him in front of me into the tent. He puts the mints down in front of Ruby. Success! He's not sweating and only slightly pink. He stands behind Ruby grinning and giving me the thumbs-up. At that moment, all of Ruby's hair at the back shoots out and attaches itself to his pullover because of the static. Luckily she doesn't notice.

At least someone's happy. Across the tent, Syd waves, taps his watch and holds up crossed fingers. I'm in despair.

Every time I try to talk to Tash she ignores me or someone interrupts. I'm gutted.

Now the lunch is finished and Syd's blasting the horn on The Tysonmobile as he guns it into the car park.

'Hel-lo, Ian. I was just telling Mr Pocky and the mayor that the precise term for the prongs on a fork is "tines". Incidentally, here's your phone.'

Great. Fat lot of use it is now.

McClaren sweeps me over to The Tysonmobile. I'll have to see Tash when I get back from the tour. It'll be my last chance. After her solo she'll be off. I can't think about what'll happen if I fail.

Terry's chatting to the mayor. In the background, there's a yell from a tourist trapped inside a collapsing Pockyloo. Terry shakes his head. 'Them tourists, we're pulling 'em out them dunnies fifteen times a day!' He chuckles and makes off for the yelling.

Syd's hurrying the Yarradindi Business Association on to The Tysonmobile before they can smell the sausage meat. He bellows nervously, 'All aborra famous tour a Yarradindi tigers, a cheeky beggas!'

I jump on. Syd jams The Tysonmobile into gear and we're off down the track.

'Fingerra crossed a tigers, a slipp'ry beggas!'

Poor Syd. This is going to be a disaster.

Terry waves from outside the First Aid Station.

I translate Syd's commentary, my mind on Tash. Syd drives The Tysonmobile into the swamp with a big splash. The mayor is making loud comments about how he's heard tiger numbers have dropped. The Tysonmobile putters past the car wrecks and churns up the slope on the other side. Syd parks, grinning anxiously. The mayor comments pointedly that we're all in for a long wait.

We sure are. We wait, then drive on a bit. Syd's gargling in panic about tigers living with cavemen. I start rattling off more commentary. Syd laughs wildly at nothing. But then, behind us, there's a rustle, a sudden blood-curdling howl and, amazingly, a tiger pads out of the bush. We gasp. The tiger stops, sniffs, bares its teeth, then starts creeping slowly and deliberately towards The Tysonmobile. People are whispering and whipping out their cameras. Syd's jubilant. Another

170

tiger appears, then another. Where are these tigers coming from?

Eight, then ten of them, then twelve, then some cubs – all creeping towards The Tysonmobile. I realize with a shock, these are Mr Frye's tigers. The smell of sausage meat from The Tysonmobile must have driven them crazy enough to escape. They've made it across the land bridge. And, by the saliva dripping from their mouths, they're clearly ravenous.

Syd's nearly exploding, trying to stifle his gargling. Cameras are snapping. But any minute now the tigers will start licking the tyres and the game will be up.

I hiss, 'Syd, get going.'

He shakes his head and chortles happily. The tigers are surrounding us, creeping closer.

'Syd, *get going*!'

The lead tiger throws back its head and gives a spine-chilling howl. They all stop. This is scary. They're looking at each other like they've got some kind of plan.

'Syd, *GO*!'

Syd jams his foot on the accelerator – a split second before the entire pack of them pounces. We roar through, scattering them. They roll over, yelp, jump up and start chasing us. They're gaining. The lead tiger leaps high in the air and hangs by its teeth from the handrail next to the mayor. Everyone screams. The mayor batters it with his shoe but it clings on. People are chucking shoes, water bottles, cameras, anything that comes to hand to put off the tigers, but nothing works. Syd rams The Tysonmobile into top gear and swerves to avoid a tree. The tiger next to the mayor drops off just as a hawk swoops down and collides with a mudguard.

'Hold onnera – vicious beggas!'

We're going so fast that seats are lurching in their brackets on every bump. We career along, crashing through the undergrowth. We come out in a clearing next to the river bank, and another hawk swoops down, just inches over everyone's heads.

I yell, 'The swamp! Go across the water! They'll lose the scent.'

Syd spins the wheel and we go hurtling through the mangroves into the river, all screaming. But the tigers throw themselves into the water behind us. They're gaining, snapping at the sides. The hawks are still dive-bombing us. They're joined by a flock of squaw-ing cockatoos. Then ibises. People are throwing themselves to the floor and yelling. An eagle lands on the steering wheel, gets battered by Syd, flaps wildly and falls off. We get to the other side and roar up the bank. The animals follow. Now we're careering at full speed up the hill. I glimpse the neat tent, all tidied. Lines of tourists are sitting peacefully on chairs set on the bright blue groundsheet. The orchestra's on the stage. I yell at them, 'Go! Go! Get going!'

They take one look, then shriek and scatter.

Pockys are running in from everywhere to try to

help. Terry bellows, 'I'll get the fire hose on the beggas!'

He charges to the Goliath 63 and hits the button. Nothing happens.

He stares down into the nozzle, bewildered. Instantly, a huge jet of high-pressure water shoots out into his face and literally knocks him off his feet.

The hose bucks out of his hand, flies up in the air, crashes down and starts snaking about like it's alive. The jet's so strong that people, tigers, music stands and chairs all get caught and sent skidding along the plastic groundsheet like it's a waterslide. There's an insane barking as Ripper, Ripperson and a pack of Pocky dogs streak out of nowhere and madly chase the tigers down the hill and back off to the swamp. For a second, Mr Frye's pinned to the tent wall yelling, 'No! No! My tigers!'

Tash is next to the stage holding her cello, soaked and yelling. And, oh God, she's wearing THAT dress. The one from the shop – the one she might pop out of at any moment. She must have changed for her solo. I have to protect her. I have to cover her up. I jump from the speeding Tysonmobile, but I can't fight through the jet to reach her.

An arc of water hits one of the Pockyloos and knocks it over. That hits another, which hits another, until four have gone over. The four tourists who were inside sit gaping through the wreckage.

Terry snatches up the hose desperately. He's

wrestling it. The jet shoots out sideways and hits Tash's cello, lifting it right out of her hands.

Not the cello . . .

23

The cello drops to the ground, rolls, gets picked up by the jet of water and spins crazily across the ground sheet. It hits the side of the stage. The neck snaps like a biscuit.

I stare in horror.

But Terry's staggering in drunken circles as he's wrenched about by the hose. He bellows, 'Switch off the pump! Switch off the pump!'

I run for the Goliath. A column of water soars from the hose up into the air. It hits the top of the marquee, catches the illegal electric cable and sends it looping down inches off the ground, like a skipping rope. It's swinging right behind Terry. But he doesn't know it's there. If he steps backwards he's dead. Dylan's five metres away, frozen in horror.

I yell, 'Dyl, the cable! Grab your dad! It's gonna electrocute him!'

As I flick off the pump, Dylan leaps through the air in a rugby tackle, pulls Terry to the ground away from the cable and the two of them, locked together, go skidding down the groundsheet, straight towards a sign reading: 'Pockys for the Planet'. Dylan crashes his head straight into the post. You actually hear him hit.

Crrrack!

For three long seconds there's absolute silence. Terry sits up, blinking, but Dylan's out cold. Everyone's staring, dripping and astonished. Next to them, the hose dribbles water. Dylan opens his eyes groggily.

One of the Yarradindi Business Association people says, 'That boy just saved his father's life. He just saved his dad from being electrocuted.'

Everyone starts cheering. Crusher and a bunch of Pocky uncles rush over to make the dangling cable safe. Dylan's beaming. Terry's slapping him on the back. Chett leans down to me and whispers, 'Good one, mate. I never thought you got the hair, but you musta done, and we got him. Yo. *Legend.*'

'Stop! Stop this! Silence!'

It's Mr Frye. He's drenched and holding up that envelope.

'I hereby make a citizen's arrest of Syd Pocky.'

Oh no. He's found out about the sausage meat.

There's dead silence. Tash is staring at her dad in dismay.

Frye glares around grimly.

'In this envelope are the results of scientific tests on the blood and droppings of the Yarradindi Tiger population two days ago. These tigers are suffering a serious Vitamin B deficiency. Pocky sausages with

176

beer and Vegemite contain extremely high amounts of yeast, which in turn contains Vitamin B. For years, the Pockys fed our tigers these sausages, making them dependent. They want to do it again. So they can exploit these defenceless animals for their own financial means. So the only reason the tigers are here today is because of . . .' he spits out the words, '. . . Pocky sausages.'

There's a silence. Frye stares round triumphantly. The audience gapes.

Terry blinks. 'Ya mean, all these years, we bin keeping them healthy?!'

'No! Yes! No, I mean, the tigers must learn how to find their own natural sources of Vitamin B . . . !'

'Ya mean, Pocky sausages are good for 'em? And when they don't have 'em they get sick?'

Mr Frye's screams are drowned out by Pocky applause and roars of approval.

'Good ol' Mr Frye!'

'Trust Mr Frye a prove a Pocky allus lookafta tigas, a cleva begga . . .'

'Three cheers for Mr Frye! Hip, hip . . .'

The entire Pocky family bellows, 'Hooray.'

Mr Frye's yelling, 'No! I didn't mean that!'

Pockys are swarming forward to shake Frye's hand. Crusher gives him the wooden Pocky Award plaque, as Terry tucks the cheque into Frye's top pocket.

Frye's yelling, 'No! Listen to me! The tigers are under serious threat!'

'Just givem more sausages, a poor beggas!'

I can't believe we just broke the cello.

It's over as quickly as it started. The tigers and birds are long since gone. Mr Frye gets carried off, protesting, by Syd and an army of excited Pocky uncles. The marquee and grounds look like a rubbish tip. Everyone's soaked. People are picking their way through the overturned orchestra chairs. Granny's trying to towel down the mayor, while Terry's got his arm around Dylan, telling anyone who'll listen how excellent he rates his son. Dylan just . . . glows.

I rush over to Tash. She's white as a sheet.

'My cello . . .'

Pricey and Bogle hurry up to us. Price takes one look at the cello, 'Whoa, priceless. We just spent fifteen hundred bucks getting it fixed and it's smashed to bits.'

Tash looks up.

'You did what?'

Oh no. Bogle covers his eyes in disbelief. Pricey blinks and realizes what he's said.

'Like . . . I mean . . .' He looks at me and mumbles, 'Sorry, mate. I'm really sorry . . .'

Tash is looking from me to Price and back again. 'You spent fifteen hundred dollars on my cello? Who did? What's been going on?'

I whisper, 'I . . . I tried to tell you. I really tried.'

'Tell me what?'

'When you asked me to pick up your cello the day music camp started. We got in a fight with the Pockys and it got run over by a truck. We took it to Mr Pilple. We paid him to fix it. I tried to tell you on the phone but . . . you didn't hear me.'

She's just staring at me.

Bogle butts in. 'He did. Honestly. He really tried. And that's why we've been working up here. All of us. Honestly.'

She blinks. 'So all that stuff about Pilple being away was lies?'

I murmur, 'Well, yeah . . .'

Price and Bogle slope discreetly away.

'And *Cemetery Trashers* was lies? And Auntie Pat?'

I nod guiltily.

'And you only helped my dad to cover that you were working here?'

'Yeah, but—'

'You took his money while you were lying to him?'

'Yeah.'

I can't read her face. Is she furious? Is she about to forgive me?

I gabble desperately. 'So you see, all the lies were for a good cause . . .'

Dead silence. My stomach somersaults. She comes to some kind of decision, takes the broken cello and walks off. I hurry after her, frantic.

'Tash! I really tried to tell you.'

'I don't know what makes you tick. Everyone else knew the truth. You didn't have the guts to tell *me* . . .'

I'm in a flat panic. 'I tried to – straight off – but you

thought I was talking about dresses. Then I was going to tell you, once I'd got it fixed, so you wouldn't worry, then you were going off with Günter and . . .'

'So it's Günter's fault now? Great. You won't even own up to your mistakes.'

This isn't fair.

'I've been working my guts out to pay for that cello!'

'Yeah, well, maybe that wasn't what I wanted. Maybe I didn't want to be treated like a child and lied to while you played some silly boys' game with your mates.'

'It wasn't a silly boys' game. I was trying to fix up what I'd wrecked.'

'If you'd just told me! Trusted me!' Her shoulders sink in exasperation. 'Ian – the cello's insured.'

I just stand there. Insured?

All this was for nothing?

Insured?

She's staring at me. 'You know, it would be really good if you said you were sorry.'

I'm stunned. 'I *did* . . . !'

'Yeah, for the cello. What about everything else?'

'I thought you'd dumped me . . .'

'You don't get it, do you? Your stupid jealousy . . . ! Günter's a friend, that's all. He's got a girlfriend in Germany he rings every night.' She's nearly in tears. 'I never wanted Günter, I wanted *you* . . .'

My head's spinning. *She never wanted Günter?*

'I could have forgiven you for breaking the cello.

It's the *lies* . . . You put me through *all that*! Worrying about Ruby, thinking you'd dumped me . . .'

I'm frantic. She never wanted Günter, she wanted me. But now it's sounding like she's finishing with me. The world's collapsing around me. What have I *done*? What can I *do*?

I'm desperate. 'But it was *for* you. For *you*. All of it, for *you*!'

I'm at my wits' end. Why can't she understand?

She looks at me for a long time, then says sadly, 'What am I to you, Rudie? Think about it.' Her eyes are searching my face. 'I was the last person who knew the truth.'

I stand, helpless.

She says quietly, 'I think it's maybe best if . . . well, we don't see each other any more.'

It's like I'm being ripped inside. I don't know what to say. That fake cheery voice comes out.

'Hey! Look! Tashie! It's not that bad, is it . . . ?'

I tail off. There's a pause and she whispers, 'Goodbye.' I mutter, 'Yeah.'

She walks off.

I watch her go, then stumble into the bush like a robot. I walk and walk, then lean against a tree.

And suddenly, I'm sobbing like a baby.

24

I ring her. She doesn't answer. I text her. I try to get messages to her through Bree. She's not interested.

Tash.

My Tashie.

She's not interested.

The days drag past. The first thing you notice is that you're empty. The second is that you start hanging about places where she is. I watch her going in and out of the town hall as the big concert approaches. My heart grabs.

Bogle and Pricey come over and we hang out. They don't know what to say, so leave. A hundred times I ask myself why I didn't tell her about the cello from the start. In five days I wrecked our relationship. I keep going over it.

But as much as I keep thinking about it, I just don't understand her. I don't understand girls, full stop. Why wasn't she pleased I tried to fix it? I mean, not even a little bit?

I write her letters. I send her a card. I watch the post for days.

No reply.

The world goes on. Our garden cafe extension gets finished and opens. Tash plays her concert at the town hall. I tell Mum and Dad that I'm going. Really I spend the time wandering on my own along the beach. Mr Frye's in the papers for discovering the connection between Pocky sausages and the tigers' health. The Pockys get to leave big troughs of sausages around the tigers' habitat to keep up their Vitamin B. Unsurprisingly, Terry never got into the Yarrandindi Business Association. He's now standing for the local council with the slogan: 'Don't think small, put Pocky in the Town Hall'. Mrs McClaren gets a new short hair cut which covers the hole in the helmet. If Chett's hex ever affected her, she never showed it. She's now head of Help our Retired Airmen – although, according to Dad, the retired airmen are putting up a spirited resistance to being helped. This consists of shouting, 'Busybody at three o'clock', and ducking into the pub every time Mrs McClaren looms into view. After all my trouble fixing up his blushing with the zapper, Price finds out that Ruby is going out with Chett Pocky (presumably for his car, but who knows?), goes right off her and starts obsessing about a hockey player from St Brigit's.

Dylan's calmed down amazingly since he's got over being jealous of Chett. He calls round to see me, claps me on the shoulder and gives me his second-best graffiti pen.

The strangest thing is, Bogle and Bree are going out together. They met at the computer mega centre on the day the new *Cemetery Trashers* was launched and hit it off like a shot. They're made for each other. I try not to be jealous of them, but it's hard.

So I don't have to see how happy they are, I stay home. I spend a lot of time playing with Daisy. Partly because she's cute, but also because she'll never ask any questions. Mum and Dad still haven't realized that I've split up with Tash.

I keep it that way.

I'm not ready for deep and meaningful chats about many more fish in the sea.

Finally, it's nine o'clock one night. We've just got rid of the last tourists.

Mum turns to me. 'Ian, can you lock the shop door, please?'

I turn the sign from 'open' to 'closed' and shove the bolt at the bottom of the door into the floor. I'm just reaching for the top bolt when out of nowhere a bunch of people loom up. It's Pilple, some woman, Mr Frye and – oh no, my heart sinks – Tash.

Pilple's grinning and banging on the door, waving a bottle of champagne and asking to be let in.

Dad looks round. 'That's that bloke Pilple, the violin maker. What's he want? Better open up for him, Ian.'

I'm writhing with embarrassment. This is absolutely

the last way I want what happened about the cello to come out.

As I open the door I snatch a look at Tash. She avoids my glance. She's as embarrassed as I am.

Pilple bursts in. 'Ian!' He slaps me on the back and turns to Dad. 'Mr Rude! Hope you're proud of that son of yours. I'm here to congratulate you and your wife, and I'm hoping you'll join my wife and myself in a glass of champagne! We wanted you, your son and his girlfriend to share in our great news. May we come in?'

Mum and Dad look at each other. They can't exactly throw him out. This is going to be horrible. Mum leads everyone through to the garden room. We all sit round a table. I try to get a chair so Tash and I don't have to look at each other, but I end up directly facing her. Her face is all hot. She still won't look at me.

Mum brings out glasses for the adults and a bottle of all-natural lemonade for me and Tash. She and Dad exchange puzzled looks. Dad folds his arms and smiles quizzically. Meanwhile, Pilple's wrestled open the bottle of champagne and is pouring it out. His wife sits next to him, beaming. I know her from somewhere, but can't work out where.

Pilple raises his glass.

'To Ian and Natasha!'

Mum and Dad are mystified, but smile and drink. I want to crawl under a stone and die. Tash has got her head tucked in so low you can see her entire parting. Pilple, his wife and Mr Frye are all grinning at me.

Pilple sets his glass down and says, 'I would like to announce three things. Number one, that my wife and I have just told Natasha and her father that we are loaning our eighteenth-century Italian cello to her for as long as she wants to play it.' Mum and Dad murmur approval. Mr Frye grins all round. 'Number two, my wife and I have now just got together again and you're all invited to a party on the twenty-fifth to celebrate.' Mum and Dad smile a bit awkwardly, but say they'd love to come. 'Number three, the person to whom my wife and I owe all this happiness is young Ian and, in grateful thanks, I am giving him a cheque for all the money he and his friends spent to repair Natasha's cello!'

Dad's bewildered. 'Cello? What's this about a cello? What repairs?'

I could die.

Mum and Dad start bombarding me with questions, but Pilple hushes them. He whips out a cheque from his pocket, makes a big show of writing it and forces me to take it.

'Thanks, Mr Pilple. I'm off now . . .'

'No, no. You mustn't go yet. I want it public and on the record. I want to tell your parents that you, Ian, and your absolute commitment to Natasha, was what gave me the courage to go back to the most important person in the world and ask her to give me another chance.'

Mum and Dad's eyebrows shoot up.

Why doesn't Pilple stop? I can't stand it. Tash's head is even lower. Frye obviously knows what Pilple's leading up to and is beaming.

'When you first came to me with that broken cello, I thought you were an irresponsible young vandal. I thought you didn't have the courage to come clean to your parents about a stupid and dangerous bit of sky-larking. I expected you to give up in a couple of days and go to them with your tail between your legs. But you didn't. You gave me all your savings . . .'

Mum and Dad's jaws drop.

'You sold all your possessions. You turned up every day, bringing your wages. Working at any job you could—'

'We all did, Mr Pilple. It wasn't just me . . .'

'But you inspired the others, Ian. And it says a lot for how much your friends think of you that they did that.'

Why won't he just *shut up*? Mum and Dad are gob-smacked. Dad tries to cut in but Pilple's going on.

'So, as the days went past, I began to think. If a boy of Ian's age can fight that hard for his relationship . . . If a boy of Ian's age can devote himself utterly, how-ever hard it is, to trying to make things right again for the person he loves—'

His wife is elbowing him. She whispers in his ear.

He looks at me then Tash in amazement and gives an uncomfortable cough.

'My wife says she thinks you two might have had a falling out. Surely not?'

Dead silence. Now Tash's arms are folded and her chin's clamped into her chest. Her whole body language is like she wishes the earth would swallow her up.

I mutter, 'Well. Yes.'

'But . . . you surely haven't split up over this cello business, have you?'

I'm dying of embarrassment. Mum and Dad are pestering me to explain. Frye's badgering Tash, who's refusing to answer. How can I get out of here?

Pilple's on again. 'But you did so much for her! I've never seen such devotion. You'd go to the ends of the earth for her . . .'

I can't stand any more of this.

I snap, 'Yeah, and I told her a pack of lies. I told everyone the truth except her. I made her look stupid in front of everyone and I didn't mean to do it, but I did, and I wrecked everything. So. I don't think I'm someone to admire or have champagne about.'

My words ring out. Nobody says anything. Tash is so hunched up her forehead's nearly touching the table. If I stay here any longer I'll either punch the wall or start crying. I storm out.

25

As I go, Pilple starts spluttering on again. He's telling Tash how I was trying to protect her feelings and there's absolutely no way I'd deliberately hurt her.

Why doesn't he mind his own business? He's just making it worse.

I stumble down the road, through the crowds of tourists. I've got to be on my own. I find myself on the beachfront. I walk and walk. The sun's going down. Finally, I'm at Tate's Point and there's nobody but me, the ocean and some surfers way off in the distance. It's getting dark. I sit down on the sand and watch the waves crash in.

Some gulls arc overhead and fly out over the water. This is where Tash and I came, the time we joked about the Wonky-Beaks. I feel like there's a hole inside me. Everything reminds me of her. Everywhere I look.

How am I ever going to get over her? And when the holidays are done and we're back in class, she'll be there every day.

I've been avoiding thinking about that, but I'll have to face it.

I'll have to watch her coming into class, sitting down, not talking to me. I'll have to see her going out with someone else.

Tears prickle in my eyes. I could have stopped it happening, I could have prevented the whole thing, but I didn't. I didn't, and now it's too late. You can kill love. You can wreck a relationship. You can do stupid things, and you look round and suddenly it's gone and nothing you do can ever get it back. You can be to blame.

It's dark. Some stars are coming out. My world is empty.

I get up and dust the sand off my hands.

The answer is that I won't get over her. At least, not for a very long time. I'll cope because I'll have to. And people do. I'll shut down. I'll tune out. Time will pass, and in time it will be OK.

But it won't.

I'm cold. Deep inside. Cold and dark.

'Ian?'

My stomach somersaults. Tash?

I turn. She's standing about ten metres away.

I stare at her. I don't know what to do. Why is she here? Is she coming back? She can't be. My heart's thumping.

She walks towards me, hesitates, then says softly, 'Rudie?'

I can hardly breathe. Now she's looking at the ground.

'I . . . I didn't know you gave up so much. I didn't

realize. I thought . . . you know, you were laughing at me. And . . . I thought, well, I thought you wanted Ruby Pearson.'

'Ruby Pearson! You've got to be kidding . . .'

We just stand there. The surf crashes.

She whispers, 'I miss you so much. I was so mean to you. Can we . . . ? Can you . . . forgive me?'

I look at her. I can feel my heart soar. I give a choked laugh.

'Forgive you? I'm the one who needs forgiving. Oh, Tash, I'm so sorry . . .'

Before I know it we're hugging and kissing. She's crying, clinging to me. I'm so happy I'm nearly crying myself.

'Tashie, you silly, stupid . . . Ruby Pearson? Are you insane? The only time she comes to life is when there are boys around she wants to flirt with. She's not a patch on you.'

'But she's so slim and good-looking. Boys find that attractive . . .'

'Where do you girls get your ideas about what boys find attractive? How do you know? Curvy is what's attractive. Interesting and warm and funny is what's attractive. Ruby's about as attractive as a bowl of week-old porridge. And about as intelligent.'

I hug her. I try to pick her up and we both fall over in the sand laughing.

'Rudie? Am I forgiven?'

'I'll consider it.'

She tickles me until I beg for mercy. We head off along the beach, arms round each other. The stars are out. In the sky to the west, there are still streaks of red. I am happy. I am so, so happy, like I can never describe, except it's as if the whole world is lit by the strongest light imaginable and everything . . . shines.

Wait a minute. Tash is talking and I'm thinking about who the Bandits will put in as half-back against the Crows this weekend!

Quick. Out of happy-male automatic pilot. Concentrate.

Listening . . . listening . . . committing to memory . . .

Tash is telling me all about Pilple and her new cello and how fantastic it is and how she would never have got it if it hadn't been for me. I glow.

'And you'll never guess, Mrs Pilple – she's the woman from the dress shop where you threw up.'

'No way . . . ! That's right, course she is. I thought I recognized her.'

'And she doesn't even seem to remember how you chucked—'

'Wait on. Hold it. What's with the "throwing up" and "chucking"? I nearly choked to death.'

'Whadever. Anyhow, she says—'

'*Whadever?* I nearly die and all you can say is, "Whadever"? I'd say that's cause for attack.'

She shoots off, shrieking. I chase after her, grab her

and do Revenge of the Wonky-Beaks until she's a giggling wreck in my arms, all soft and cuddly and warm.

'No, but Rudie, listen . . .' She's got her hands on my shoulders, staring deep into my eyes. 'The best thing. She's said I can have any dress in the place for half price. I mean, how cool is that? I'm going tomorrow. So . . .' she beams, 'coming with me?'

I gaze into her dazzling face.

'Am I coming shopping? For dresses?'

She's smiling at me. She is the smartest, most interesting, most gorgeous girl in the world. I will promise to trust her. I will promise not to tell stupid lies or panic that she'll dump me. I will promise not to feel I have to fix all her problems like she's a little child. Bottom line, I will walk over hot coals for her.

But shopping for dresses? When she turns into Mad Woman of the Changing Cubicle, and I become Disaster Man?

I peck a kiss on that lovely mouth.

'Absolutely, utterly . . . NO!'

Also by Linda Aronson –

Ian Rude's first adventures . . .

RUDE
HEALTH

Ian Rude's life is an embarrassment – hardly
surprising with a name like his. Plus he's short, he's
accident-prone and his parents run a health-food shop.
Things really couldn't get much worse – could they?

Does Ian have secret superhuman powers?
Are his mum's Teenage Energy Tablets (with
odourless garlic) stronger than she realizes?

Plain Rude

When Ian pretends he's seriously into conservation
in order to get Suzie, the most gorgeous girl at school,
to notice him, he doesn't count on being blackmailed
by nature-mad Natasha. Looking after Natasha's
snot-spitting bats is bad enough, but things get
desperate when she wants him to sabotage the
Pockys' new emu farm.

Will Ian get the gorgeous Suzie or will demented
Natasha drown him in Syd Pocky's toilet bowl first?

And another brilliant book from Linda Aronson

Kelp

Emily wants to be the world's youngest self-made millionaire. Instead, she's stuck on a tiny island with her eccentric family and their slimy, smelly seaweed factory. Her only ray of hope is a gorgeous hunk with a mobile phone and A LOT of money. Trouble is, she hasn't met one . . . yet.

A selected list of titles available from Macmillan Children's Books

The prices shown below are correct at the time of going to press. However, Macmillan Publishers reserves the right to show new retail prices on covers, which may differ from those previously advertised.

Linda Aronson

Rude Health	978-0-330-39060-1	£4.99
Plain Rude	978-0-330-48254-7	£4.99
Kelp	978-0-330-36949-7	£4.99

Terence Blacker

Boy2Girl	978-0-330-41503-3	£4.99

Frank Cottrell Boyce

Framed	978-0-330-43425-6	£5.99
Millions	978-0-330-43331-0	£5.99

Andy Griffiths

The Day My Bum Went Psycho	970-0-330-40089-3	£4.99

Eva Ibbotson

The Beasts of Clawstone Castle	978-0-330-43425-2	£4.99

Alex Williams

The Talent Thief	978-0-330-44352-4	£5.99

All Pan Macmillan titles can be ordered from our website, www.panmacmillan.com, or from your local bookshop and are also available by post from:

Bookpost, PO Box 29, Douglas, Isle of Man IM99 1BQ
Credit cards accepted. For details:
Telephone: 01624 677237
Fax: 01624 670923
Email: bookshop@enterprise.net
www.bookpost.co.uk
Free postage and packing in the United Kingdom